pretty little WEREWOLF

KATIE SALIDAS

Pretty Little Werewolf
ISBN 978-1-7321014-0-1
Copyright © 2015 by Katie Salidas

Cover Art by
https://www.wegotyoucoveredbookdesign.com/

Published by:
Rising Sign Books
http://www.KatieSalidas.com

For more information about my books email:
katiesalidas@gmail.com

Books by Katie Salidas

The Immortalis Series
Becoming a Vampire is easy. Living with the condition is the hard part.
Carpe Noctem
Hunters & Prey
Pandora's Box
Soulstone
Dark Salvation

Olde Town Pack
Werewolf romances to make your pulse race and heart pound.
Moonlight
Mated
Being Alpha

Chronicles of the Uprising
Dystopian thrillers with a Paranormal twist.
Dissension
Complication
Revolution
Transition
Retribution
Annihilation

Little Werewolf Series
A Coming of Age Wolf Shifter Adventure.
Pretty Little Werewolf
Curious Little Werewolf
Fearless Little Werewolf

1

Nerves frayed worse than the ends of her shoelaces she kept picking at, Giselle Richards was in no fit state to deal with people, but that didn't matter. As a minor, her life was dictated by the will of others.

Breathe. Just breathe. Giselle closed her eyes as the taxi cab came to a stop. She focused on centering herself, controlling her breath, being in the moment. Yoga had never really been her thing, but she did appreciate the way the breathing exercises helped to calm her wilder side. And today of all days, she needed that control. Walking in with hands jittery and shaking would be a dead giveaway of her nerves and, with a reputation preceding her, that would just confirm what everyone had to suspect – that she was a freak.

Never let them see you scared. Never let them know you're weak. A mantra ingrained into the very fabric of her being. Life was tough for Giselle, and she had to be tougher. No matter how much she wanted to run screaming into the open desert. No. She had to go in appearing confident, with her head held high.

One breath at a time, in and out. Slowly. Easy enough,

normally. Today, however, not so much. And not just because of where she was. All it took was a quick glance up at the sky and she spotted it, in broad daylight: the beautiful roundness of the moon. Even now it called to her. It would be full come evening. The worst kind of monthly visitor a girl could ever have. And it had to happen on this day.

New home day.

Just outside of the taxi cab stood the house that would become her new home. However long it lasted. Maybe a week or two… maybe less, after the moon had its way with her.

She'd like to imagine she'd live there longer. Great big two-story home. Probably four or five bedrooms inside. Maybe one of her very own. Now that was dreaming a bit too high. New room or not, the house looked nice, and obviously loved. Christmas lights strewn all over the yard were blinking in time with music. And Frosty and all his winter friends were waving from the curb. If only there were snow to complete the winter wonderland. Still, even without it, this home looked like a dream, with warm and loving people ready to invite her into their family. But Giselle knew better.

"You'll see. This place will be wonderful," Mrs. Perkins, her counselor said, a little too enthusiastically.

Giselle rolled her eyes, already feeling the pull of the moon calling her wolf to rise to the surface. Dealing with Mrs. 'Perky' Perkins was bad enough on a normal day… She really had to control her breathing today. Jenny Perkins just had to place her right away. Couldn't hold out for a day longer. If she only knew how wrong she was.

Mrs. Perkins' lips pulled tight with disappointment. "Oh, don't be like that. This place will be wonderful."

"You said that already."

What the hell did that woman know anyway? She didn't

have kids, and was certainly not a child of the system. Nor was she a freak of nature. Sitting there in her pretty pink pants suit with perfect blonde hair. Perfect nails. Perfectly stylish shoes. Perfect life to match, probably. If Giselle rolled her eyes any harder, they'd pop out and get lost under her seat.

"Fine, then. That sour puss is not going to help your situation any, but you're still going in there and meeting your new foster family."

The front door of the house opened, and Giselle watched a woman step outside. She spotted the cab and cracked a smile, but as soon as the she stepped off of the front porch, caution replaced eagerness and she took her time walking toward the car. Tall for a woman. Thin, but hiding it behind the bulk of winter clothes. She might have been mid-forties, Giselle couldn't quite tell, but she moved with the grace of a younger woman. The look on her face, though, was more than cautious. She was worried, and trying to hide it.

Great. Just great! Here we go again. Breathe. You can do this.

Giselle's reputation had already preceded her. How could it not? She might not even last the night let alone the holiday season at this house. *Problem child. Weirdo. Freak.* The echoes of all the terrible things she'd been called came back to haunt her, stealing some of her resolve. She fit all of the above and then some, sure, but it was wholly another thing to be called them. Hurtful as they were, she understood normal people's fear. When you wolfed out once a month, literally, you couldn't expect anyone, even the most well-meaning of families, to accept you.

Shuffled from one foster home to the next, she'd seen one too many a house like this: pretty to look at, but never meant to be hers. Her life had been turned upside down in the last three years. Growing up had brought more changes than she had bargained for. Most girls only had to worry about boobs and training bras during their pre-teen years. Maybe a few awkward days with stained clothes. She'd gotten all those gifts – and the added bonus of growing a bushy tail and a set of impressive canines each cycle. And as soon as that started, so had the revolving door of foster homes. Sure, they were all happy and welcoming at first; until they saw what kind of a freak she truly was. Then it was a race to get rid of her.

At least they'd been good enough to keep silent about her condition as they shuffled her back into the care of her caseworkers. 'It just didn't work out' became her catch-phrase.

Hiding her abnormality bought her a few months, but even then, someone would get wise and it was, "Sorry, but you need to leave." Same old song, only the tempo of it seemed to increase each time it was played.

"You planning on living in there?" The woman, her new foster parent asked, gazing expectantly though the car window.

Could she? Only two years left until freedom. Two more years until she was aged out of the system and on her own as an adult. If only.

"Sorry." Giselle took one last centering breath, trying to rein in her nerves, and opened the car door. The moment the crisp air hit her nose, she picked up on an odd fragrance. Strangely comforting, though she couldn't exactly say why. She'd definitely smelled it before, but couldn't place it. Earthy and rich. Like dirt after a storm, yet the ground was bone dry. Vegas hadn't seen rain in well over a month, and the front yard of this house, and all the houses on this street, minus the festive decorations, was rock. Desert landscaping. So where was the smell coming from? She'd have to figure that out another time. Jenny was already pushing her bags out of the car behind her.

"Be good, Giselle!" she said a bit too enthusiastically. "Martina? Dear, the paperwork has been faxed over. Have fun!"

"C'mon then. Let's get you inside. It's a bit chilly out here and these old bones don't like cold." The woman, Martina, turned a quick glance at Jenny who hadn't bothered to get out of the car. "We'll take good care of her."

"I'll be around. Call if you need me." She tapped the driver on the shoulder and before another word was said, the car pulled away.

'Shocked' was an understatement. Giselle had been dropped off quickly before, but the speed with which Jenny had left made her head spin. Did she know something about this home that Giselle didn't? Why hadn't she walked her inside and completed the stacks of paperwork that normally accompanied a transfer like this? If anything, Giselle suspected it was the fact she knew she'd be back tomorrow to take her to the girls' home when this Martina lady freaked out over her... condition. Yeah. That must be it. No point in making more paperwork for yourself.

"In a hurry, that one." Martina laughed and ushered her up the path to the house. "Only the one bag?"

"I travel light." Only because she'd never stayed anywhere long enough to accumulate junk to pack. Keeping her head up, Giselle followed Martina's lead, trying to maintain her calming breaths.

The inside of the house was just as she'd imagined: large and open, with a big fireplace, comfortable sofa, and even a big cushy reclining chair. An L-shaped high island separated the kitchen from the living room but still gave the feel of being part of the open space. Off to the far wall was a steep staircase with a white bannister. A girl could get used to all this space. And before she could wonder aloud if there were any other kids there, Martina shouted from the bottom of the stairs, "Come and say hello to our new girl, Giselle."

That answered that question, but gave her even more to be worried about. Keeping parents from learning her secret was difficult enough, but other kids… no way.

Martina must have caught the apprehension on Giselle's face, because she guided her over to the cushy recliner and had her sit.

"Don't look so worried. We don't bite."

If she hadn't already been on edge, Giselle might have laughed at the joke. They might not – but she certainly did.

"You already know I'm Martina. My husband is Gavin. He'll be home later. Working late at the housing development. We've got two other girls under this roof, my adopted loves, like you. It's a packed house, but we always make it work. You'll all love each other."

Five people was not a packed house. Especially with all this space. She could really stretch her legs out here. The 'make it work' part had her snorting a little. "Thanks." She really didn't know what to say. No point in being too friendly to people who would probably kick her out within the month, if not that very evening when the moon came to call.

"Don't talk much, do you?" Martina asked. The curious way she eyed Giselle said she wanted to pry but knew better. A fact Giselle was quite thankful for. She shrugged, again not having anything to add to the conversation.

Martina wandered into the kitchen and poured a glass of water. "Well, that's fine. You'll need some adjustment time, I'm sure. Thirsty?"

Giselle shook her head.

Thunderous rumbling started overhead and traveled the length of the ceiling.

"That'll be the girls now. They've been eager to see who

we'd get."

When the noise reached the stairs, Giselle saw two sets of feet barreling down into the living room.

With the way Martina spoke and the enthusiastic stomping down the stairs, you'd have thought they were getting a puppy for Christmas. Giselle snickered silently. *If only they knew the truth.*

Two girls, her age by the looks of them, circled her, not bothering with words yet. They were clearly busy scrutinizing every inch of her. Each one looked as if she was trying desperately to be a cover model for *Teen Fashion.* – a far cry from Giselle's grunge-inspired attire. Chalk that up as yet another reason she was not going to fit in.

"Pay up, Taylor, I said redhead!" The tallest and thinnest of the girls laughed. She was wearing a pair of uber-trendy black slouchy boots with leggings, shorts, and a chunky purple and gray knit sweater that Giselle wondered if she might be able to borrow sometime later… assuming she did stay past the full moon. The blonde looked as if she'd just stepped off the page of the magazine Giselle had been reading on the drive over. She held out a hand with impeccably manicured nails and snatched a five-dollar bill from the girl to her left.

The loser didn't look much like she cared. "You always say redhead, Di. Bound to be right sometime." She shrugged and turned her eyes on Giselle. "Be honest, do you dye it?"

Taken aback by the question, Giselle had no words. She shook her head.

Just as trendy, the girl who'd lost the bet was wearing a blue sweater dress, belted at the waist, that matched the color of her eyes. She plopped herself on the edge of the seat and flipped back her brunette hair. "That's Diana right there," she pointed to the blonde girl with the slouchy boots. She's always right."

Giselle snorted. Ring leader. Every place has one.

"And I'm Taylor," Taylor smiled brightly. "And you are?"

Not ever going to fit in with this crowd. "Are we really doing this?" Giselle rolled her eyes. She hadn't planned for the inquisition, or to be sent to a house with fashionistas in training.

"Don't be so rude, new girl!" Di's tone turned sour.

"What's the problem here?" Worry – or maybe just annoyance, Giselle couldn't tell – had darkened Martina's tone.

"No problem. Just don't need the whole let's pretend we're all cool with each other kumbaya crap."

"Language!" Martina gave her a warning look, and Giselle's inner wolf rose up defensively.

"Crap's not a bad word." She had to hold back the snarl as her wolf clawed up closer to the surface. She'd need to get out and run soon. Burn away this pent up anxiety and stress.

"In this house, we speak respectfully to each other." Martina met her eyes with all the strength of an Alpha. Giselle felt it and her wolf too seemed to recognize it, wanting even more now to show its own strength and dominance.

There was something more to Martina; Giselle felt it deep within her. The way her wolf responded to Martina's attempt at parental dominance. There was more below the surface. But what? She couldn't quite put a finger on it. If she stayed, she'd get to the bottom of it. However, she was already on the wrong foot, pissing off the family within ten minutes of her arrival. A new record. Bonus points in the game of 'how fast could she get herself kicked out.'

"Fine," she sighed, and remembered her breathing to

help push the feelings down. After a moment, she was able to send her wolf to rest with a silent promise that she could come out that evening, no matter what. For now, though, she needed to play happy family.

"It's okay." Martina's warning glare softened, and the whole mood of the room calmed. "I understand. You've been through a few homes, and that can be quite a painful experience. It's only natural you would be defensive and guarded. But we're different here. Give it a chance. Give us a chance. You'll see."

The girls all seemed to soften their judgmental glares as well, as if Martina had given them all a silent command to be nice. Giselle wasn't about to question it, but things were feeling a bit too Stepford Wives in the house at that moment.

She wasn't buying it, and the moon's pull seemed to have taken over her tongue. "I've heard it before. You're the friggin' Brady Bunch. Whatever. Look. Just show me to my bed and let me be alone."

Gah! Why couldn't she just play nice? Giselle gave herself a mental kick in the ass, and when she found Martina's angry face again staring down at her, she knew she'd screwed up. Martina could look positively scary when she was mad.

"I'll take you to where you will sleep, but no one is ever alone here. Of that I can assure you."

She just needed to find a calm quiet place to rein it all back in. A few moments of peace. Giselle stood, and Martina waved a hand to the stairs. "Up this way, please."

She didn't bother looking at the girls as she walked away, certain she'd pissed them off. They might have been nice, but friendship was pointless.

"Be as grumpy as you like for now. I understand what you are going through." Martina's words were soft-spoken with sincerity, but Giselle had been burned too many times.

She said nothing in response; just kept on walking as Martina led her down the hall to a room on the left with two bunk beds inside. "You're on the bottom bunk on the right. I didn't know what colors you liked, so I had the girls help me set up the bed for you."

Giselle smirked at the pink nightmare in front of her. And lace! Who the hell wanted to sleep on anything with lace? A toddler version of Martha Stewart must have designed this bed space. It was truly horrid, but despite her revulsion, Giselle sighed, saying, "It's fine. Thanks," and tossed her bag on the bed before setting herself down too. Anything to get rid of Martina and have a few minutes to collect herself and send her wolf to rest again.

"I'll be just downstairs if you need anything. Dinner is at six. Lights out at nine." Martina smiled and tried to make eye-contact with Giselle, but she quickly looked away and flopped down on the bed.

"I'm not hungry."

"I didn't ask if you were. Dinner is at six and we will all eat… or at the very least, sit together."

"Fine."

"See you then." Martina pulled the door closed.

2

Dinner had been no less awkward, but Giselle had made a good effort to avoid biting someone's head off through the incessant questions about her past and why she'd been in the system. They'd been particularly interested in how she'd ended up there. But Giselle had never known her parents. Never knew where she came from. She wasn't from Vegas, either. She'd been shipped over after her first bad month three years before. Previous foster parents had been traumatized and wanted her as far away as humanly possible. She'd never liked Vegas. Too dry, too much desert. No forests. She missed the green and trees of Oregon. Thinking about what she had lost made her feel even more on edge. When she'd run up stairs crying, something Giselle had never done, least of all in front of people, Martina took pity on her and asked the other girls to stay downstairs for the night so she could adjust to her new environment in peace.

A small but very much appreciated gesture by Martina. There was something very comforting about that woman. Sure, they all said they understood, but Martina was almost empathetic in her dealings with Giselle. Maybe she'd been a kid in the system growing up too? Either way, Giselle appreciated the alone time, especially with the moon playing havoc with her mood.

The bedroom window overlooked the backyard, and she spied a small gate that led behind the houses. An alleyway. Not something she was used to seeing, but it gave her an idea. She could hop down onto the pergola and then to the ground easy enough. Climbing back up wouldn't be that hard either. And that back gate would make an easy exit. There was plenty of open desert around; she'd noticed it on the way into the neighborhood. If she was lucky, she could sneak out for a run and be back without anyone else finding out.

The moon's silvery light called, not to her but to her wolf, urging it to rise to the surface and take over. The promise of freedom and the wind through her hair was temping to both Giselle and her wolf. No. Not just temping – nearly irresistible. Trying to ignore the call of the wolf only ended up causing her to lash out like a banshee at everyone and everything around her. PMS had nothing on a wolf trying to claw its way to the surface. She'd surely be sent off to the nut house if that happened… again. Her decision had been made before she'd had the chance to question the *what if*s of being caught.

She had to do it. Just one quick run. Let the transformation calm the beast. Her wolf responded at just the thought of rising up, whimpering and begging.

Run. Freedom. Now.

Giselle listened for sounds coming from the floor below. The family, from what she could hear, were settling in to watch a movie. The heavenly scent of popping corn and butter rose up through the floor and she salivated, wondering if she might get some when she returned. She'd have at least an hour, maybe more, while they were entertained, and maybe she'd join them after… just for a snack, if there was any popcorn left.

With that thought, Giselle disrobed and unlocked the window. She dove down to the patio cover and bounded off it to the concrete below. With a quick glance back to make sure she hadn't alerted the others, Giselle took a deep breath and allowed the transformation to take hold. Her wolf came to the surface, rising and spreading to every inch of her limbs. Hair sprouted in thick tufts, covering her naked form. She shrank down, bones popping as they re-formed. Her face contorted, mouth and nose elongating, fangs descending though her gums. To an outsider the process might look painful, but the melding of her inner animal with her human form was actually freeing and completely painless. In fact, she felt more at peace with herself in her animal form, letting the wolf take control and guide her. The burdens of the world didn't matter when she was the wolf. Only the freedom to run and the wind through her fur mattered.

Shaking off the last of her transformation, Giselle bounded off through the back gate and down the street, looking for the desert that lay just behind their neighborhood.

The crisp air was heaven blowing through her fur, and the dirt under her paws was soft like powder. This was freedom. This was what made life worth living. If only she could stay this way forever. The wolf was more *her* than the human. She could hunt and fend for herself; she only needed a small den to live in. The thought was more than tempting, and as she fantasized, a jackrabbit crossed her path. The little furball was fast, and a game of chase was just what Giselle needed to take her mind away. Zigging this way and that, hopping over rocks and dodging tall cacti, the chase made everything that much more fun. She almost caught the little hopper when that same familiar cloying scent caught in her nose. Again, just like before, it perplexed her. Unusual and at the same time calming in nature, it smelled like… home. Not the building in which she might now reside, but the feeling associated with comfort and companionship. How it all translated made no sense to her, but her wolf immediately joined the smell with the feeling. Home. Familiar. Another wolf, or more. A pack.

Her wolf had it all sorted, but Giselle still couldn't locate the source. Where was the cloying moist dirt coming from, when there was nothing but dry desert around? Damn it! And now she'd lost the rabbit.

No matter, she didn't need to eat. Dinner with Martina had been satisfying enough. As she looked around, getting a lay of the land, she spotted the glow of the Luxor light. Even now, as far from the Strip as she was, the light shone brightly like a beacon into the sky. Surrounding it was the colorful glow from the nearby casinos. Vegas was unlike any other place she had ever lived. Both a magical playground of temptation and greed and then, beyond those borders, a normal suburban city like any other town in the USA. The duality of it was what made it so unique.

The smell again played with her senses, but no matter where she looked, she couldn't spot a source. That didn't stop her wolf, though. She took off at a trot, meandering though the cactus and dry grass, following the scent this way and that.

A lone wolf howled to the left of her. At least, she thought it was a lone wolf. A moment later another howl came from her right. Then again in front of her. She crouched down behind a small tuft of dry grass and peered through the blades, looking for the owner of that last howl. The smell of cloying dirt grew stronger. She picked up on the sound of paws padding toward her. Whoever they were, and there were most certainly more than one of them, surrounding her; and they would be on her, quick.

The first one came at her from the left, a gray and black wolf. It stopped just three feet away, close enough for Giselle to really pick up on the scent. That was it. She was smelling other wolves. Werewolves... like her. She didn't need to see the shift to know. She just did. It was in the eyes: the intelligence of something more than just animal. The rest of the pack, four wolves in all, in varying colors from winter white to solid black, surrounded her, no one making an aggressive move... yet. They stood, ready for action, but kept their attention on the wolf directly in front of Giselle.

The two toned wolf shifted, taking on human form, Martina's form, in front of her. "Giselle. Can you control your shift yet?"

Giselle crouched and a growl rumbled up her throat. She'd wondered at the connection, but never dared to dream of the possibilities. How could this be? That question splintered into hundreds. She'd never met someone like herself. Never. And now, not only was she among her own kind, but more than one... a pack.

Martina lowered herself to her knees, then to her hands, till she was eye level with Giselle. "It's okay. I am just like you. We all are. We mean no harm." She held a hand out, palm up for Giselle as a sign of good faith that she was here in peace.

Every instinct told Giselle to back away and run. This couldn't be happening; and yet, it was. A pack. A real wolf pack. People of her own kind. There had to be a catch. There was always a catch.

"I'm guessing you haven't learned control yet," Martina said. "Not surprising, seeing how you've been shuffled around. That's okay. We all have to learn sometime. Please trust me. I can help."

Giselle had learned to control the shift years ago, but

rather than give away her strengths, she let Martina guide her. She was still testing the waters; still wrapping her head around the fact that all she had dreamed about had come true.

"Just relax. Breathe slowly and remember what your human form feels like. Send your wolf back to rest."

There was no reason not to shift now. Martina was no immediate threat. And questions needed to be answered. Giselle shifted and stood. "When did you know? How did you know? Why didn't you say something?"

Martina laughed. "Now she speaks."

"Do you blame me?"

Martina held her hands out to hug Giselle but did not step forward. "No, child, I don't. You've had it rough. To be tossed around in the system because of what you are. I can only imagine the anger and distrust within you. If you'd come to us with anything less than anxiety, I'd wonder at your character. But it's okay now. You're among kin."

"I don't know what that means."

"You will. Trust me. We're going to make things better for you. You have a pack – this pack. If you want it. These girls and my husband, we were all lone wolves once."

"You'll have to excuse me if I am not quick to trust." Giselle did not accept the offer of a hug. She stood her ground, eyeing Martina suspiciously.

Martina dropped her arms and smiled. "I'd expect no less from a potential Alpha."

Alpha? No. Giselle was no leader. She was a lone wolf. "If you knew, then why didn't you say something earlier?"

"You needed to meet us this way. It was the only way."

Deep within her, Giselle knew she was right. Her wolf needed to see with its own eyes the others. They needed to meet on equal footing. Only then would both halves of the same person be able to truly embrace the possibilities this new revelation would bring. Though what to do with this new information was a bit of a conundrum. Never before had she imagined being with or even close to a full-fledged pack. The possibilities, though promising, had her human side cautious. She'd been burned so many times before by allowing hope to guide her. "And now that I have?"

"You can decide what to do about it."

"Meaning?"

"Join us, if you will." Martina spoke plainly, but the other wolves around her yipped with approval.

"I need time."

"Of course. But for now, let's not waste the night. The moon is calling. Run with us." Martina shifted back before Giselle could answer and took off with the rest of the pack in tow.

Giselle couldn't resist the offer of a moonlight run. She called her wolf forward, shifted, and took off after the others.

3

Two weeks in a home with wolves like her was more than Giselle had ever hoped for. She felt like she had finally found her niche. She could be herself without hiding. No more excuses, no more lies, no more feeling like a freak when her secret inevitably came out. And best of all... no more packing her bags.

Years of struggle with who she was melted away as she began to see that life did not always have to revolve around watching your back for the next person to screw you over or leave you cold in the street. There was hope.

She'd grown to really enjoy being surrounded by other wolves, and dreaded the end of the winter break. The end of vacation meant one more hurdle she'd have to overcome on the road to the perfect new life now within her grasp... a new school.

Diana scooped up her arm and pulled her along the path towards the school office. "C'mon. Depression and defensiveness don't look good on you. This will be fine. Remember, you're not a lone wolf anymore. We got your back."

Giselle had to admit, it was nice being part of a built-in

clique… and a trendy one at that. She'd never had such nice and fashionable clothes before. And her new family was more than willing to help her fill in all the gaps she'd had in the past. Hair, makeup, clothes, jewelry… she'd never had such nice things. She was spoiled… and liked it, though she did hold on to her flannel shirts. You never knew when grunge would come back. All trends were cyclical. At least that was the reason she gave the girls when they threatened to burn her old things in the bonfire to celebrate the New Year.

"I'd still prefer homeschool," Giselle said, allowing Di to drag her inside the large brick building, which looked more like a prison than a school. All the way through the corridors and even into the courtyard, the place had a very two-tone, institutional feel. Neat walkways, lockers that blended in with the brick work, hardly a sign or bit of personalization to be found, except for the bulletin board in the center of the yard with flyers for the various clubs and special meetings. That was the only bit of real color in the place.

Thank the gods she only had two years in this place before she'd be off to college. Community, probably, unless she could qualify for some scholarship money, but dreams were few and far between and she'd blown her karmic wad on the new family she'd lucked into.

Still, the prospects were looking up – although not at this particular moment as she walked into the main office and found a sour-faced lady manning the counter.

"Giselle Richards, new transfer," she said as politely as she could.

Di stood by, checking her makeup with a small compact mirror.

"You have any paperwork for me?" the sour-faced woman asked.

Giselle rummaged through her bag and pulled out a folder. "I believe it's all here."

The woman took it, gave a quick glance at the contents, and tapped a few keys on her computer. "Richards, you said?"

It was right there on the damn paperwork in front of her… Couldn't she just look herself? Giselle took a calming breath. *Be good. Be nice. It's the first day*, she chanted to herself, and then forced a smile on her face and nodded.

A printer behind the woman fired out a few quick pieces of paper, and she snatched them up just as fast. "Here's your locker assignment, code, and class schedule. Have your teachers sign off on each page and return it at the end of today."

"Thank you." Giselle grabbed her schedule, happy to be able to leave the office, and she and Di made their way through the packed hallway toward her locker.

"I just need to grab my things and I'll be right back to take you to Chem, okay?" Di said, leaving her at the locker.

"I'll be fine. I don't need a babysitter." Giselle let her eyes wander off down the hallway… where they landed on drool-worthy candidate to help her take her mind off of Di's overbearing assistance. He must have felt her staring because the moment she settled on him, he looked over and flashed her a smile. Dirty blond hair, either teased or blown out – not that she thought boys did that – but either way, those wind-swept locks suited him. And so did the longer sideburns too. A little retro, but they framed his face so well. And when his puppy-dog brown eyes met hers, she couldn't help but smile back. Maybe there would be some good things about this school after all.

Di's voice broke through her daydream of chatting up Mr. Puppy-Dog Eyes. "You're going to let me help you around today, Elle. I won't hear any arguments about it."

Di's domineering tone was beginning to grate on Giselle's nerves, especially when it invaded her fantasies. Good intentions aside, Di needed to tone it down, and if she didn't do it soon, Giselle would have to say something, as her wolf was already on edge. For now though, she tried to remind herself that this was what families did… take care of each other, no matter how intrusive they were in the process. Something she'd need to get used to if she was going to be part of a family. She sighed and turned to open her locker. "Whatever, Di. Help if you must, but don't baby me."

If Di heard her, she didn't respond. Not that Giselle needed verbal confirmation; she turned back around and slammed her locker shut without looking, and then stumbled straight into something… someone… hard.

"Oh, sorry," Giselle mumbled, trying to steady herself. She hadn't caught the scent until after she looked up and saw who she'd almost knocked down – or, well, collided with. She couldn't have knocked him down if she'd tried.

Hello, Boy!

He was magnificent. Was every guy in this school a male model? Towering over her at well above six foot, with muscles that went on for days, he was built like a statue with a hard jaw and stone-cold eyes to match. Though his looks were definitely worth paying attention to, it was his smell that had her standing dumbfounded. In all the years since she'd first experienced the change, she had never run into anyone like her. Now, standing here right in front of her was yet another wolf. She'd thought the lingering scent of wet earth might have been left in Di's wake, but the longer he stood here, looking down at her, the stronger the smell got.

"Do you have a problem?" he asked with a voice that complemented that spectacular body of his. Smooth and deep. Seriously… what a package. Her wolf was definitely at attention and begging for a second to come to the surface for a closer inspection. It was all she could do not to wolf out right there in the hallway, with all the students around to see. Yeah. That would make for a great first impression.

Hiya, everyone… I'm the new girl, and… oh, yeah, and I'm a wolf, too. She might as well tape an old "Kick me" sign on her back; it would be less conspicuous.

While she was practically drooling where she stood, the strange boy, wolf, man –whatever he was – looked positively murderous. "Are you going to stand here all day, or can I get to my locker?"

So much for making a good first impression on him. "Sorry." Giselle cleared her throat, wanting to say something smart, but for once, she didn't have the words. She sidestepped sheepishly, and enjoyed the back view of him as he brushed past her to his own locker.

Damn. Nice butt.

Her wolf agreed, too. *Wonder what his wolf looks like. I'll show you mine if you show me yours!* She couldn't help but stare. How often did she run into other wolves? Male wolves. Other than Gavin, Martina's mate, she'd never met another male wolf.

Try as she might, she couldn't stop staring. His body created a gravitational pull that her eyes couldn't break free from.

"What are you doing?" Di snatched Giselle by the arm and pulled her away with the urgency of rescue worker trying to save a child from a burning building.

Giselle pulled her arm out of Di's grasp, growling at the way she being manhandled. The last time she'd been yanked around like that was when her first family had learned of her abnormality. She hadn't liked it then, and she wouldn't tolerate it now. "Grab me like that again, and

I'll…"

The shocked look on Di's face said more than words, but she still apologized anyway. "Sorry. I didn't mean to… Look. Stay away from Asher."

Giselle took a calming breath to dampen the bark of her tone. "Why didn't you tell me there were more here?"

"Because not all of them are friendly."

To be fair, she had bumped into Asher, so he was well within rights to be grumpy with her, but she hadn't thought he was overly mean in their short meeting. If anything, she'd made a fool of herself and it was kind of Asher to not have made a public spectacle of her.

"Just stay away from him… and his pack." Di's adamant warning made Giselle all the more curious.

Of course, never having met any others of her kind, she couldn't understand the stress Di was putting on the situation. OK, so there were more wolves, and no doubt packs were a bit territorial, but the animal was only half of what they were. As people, they were rational and could accept sharing of one another's territory. Couldn't they? So what could make two packs in close proximity hate each other? The mystery of it made her all that much more curious.

"Whatever." She shrugged off Di's warning for the moment, determined to dig deeper in her own time, and allowed Di to walk next to her to Chemistry.

Di switched subjects immediately, and the whole way down the corridor she rambled on about something to do with shopping and purses, things that under normal circumstances might have interested Gisele; but her mind was locked on Asher and the possibility of meeting more of her kind.

"…and then we'll hit the mall after school to pick you up a new outfit, okay?" Di had the look of someone expecting an answer, but Giselle couldn't remember the question.

"Yeah. Let's do that." She smiled awkwardly, hoping she had given the right answer.

Di's eyes narrowed. Apparently not what she'd hoped to hear. "We'll talk about it more at lunch." She said a bit impatiently.

"Great!" Giselle ducked into her classroom, thankful to have an excuse to walk away before the angry glare turned into more. "Later."

Chemistry. Not her best subject, and to have it first thing in the morning was going to make for a fun remainder of the school year. She glanced around the classroom, taking in all the beakers and Bunsen burners and test tubes neatly organized on the counters. The cupboards with glass doors had all manner of vials and bottles behind them. She said a silent prayer she wouldn't accidentally blow anything up and embarrass herself. Then, as her eyes left the equipment, she found the handsome puppy-dog-eyed boy from the hallway. He was staring right at her. She smiled coyly and tried as best she could to say hello with her eyes.

The teacher spotted her and called Giselle over. "You're my newbie, I take it." He didn't look much like she'd expected a chemistry teacher to be. Maybe she had seen too many sci-fi shows, but she'd kind of hoped for an eccentric Doc Brown vibe. Instead, she got an early thirties, straight laced, blazer wearer with slick back hair and a plastic smile. "Packed house here. You can take the open spot at Ash's table. Second row to the left."

She looked in the direction he pointed and spotted the hot wolf boy she'd stepped on in the hallway. This class was turning out to be hottie central. *Hello, again… wolf boy!*

"Need me to make introductions, or is that too embarrassing?" The teacher asked.

"No, thanks, I'm good."

"Good, I hate mindless chatter. I'm Mr. Harper. Only call on me when you are really confused. Otherwise, shut up and listen. Got it?"

Definitely not what she'd expected from a teacher. But though his dominant tone irked her wolf, she would not allow the beast to ruin her first day. Giselle nodded and headed toward her seat. A quick glance sideways at Asher brought a smile to her face she just couldn't hide. He was a wolf, all right, but more than that, he was a really hot guy. Hot with a capital H. And that made Di's warning all that much more tempting to break.

"Sorry I stepped on your toe back there."

He grunted, if that could be considered a reply. Maybe he was more wolf than boy. Having not met any male werewolves other than Gavin, who really wasn't around much, it was entirely possible they were just brutish beings dressed up like humans. She really hoped not. It would be a shame to waste such a hot body if that were the case.

"I'm new here. Don't mean to make enemies my first day, you know." Giselle hated small talk, but really wanted to get him to say something, and found herself stumbling over her words.

He didn't answer.

"So, it's like that, then?" she asked. Either he was really mad at her, or there was something else going on. He wasn't even bothering to look in her direction with his non-responding grunts. Maybe Di was right about him.

"Miss.... Richards? New girl!" Mr. Harper called out loud enough to get the whole class's attention. "Is there something you need to say? Should we all wait for you to finish chatting up Mr. Thrace, or is it okay for me to teach now?"

Nothing like mortifying embarrassment to ease into the

treacherous waters of high school. Thank you, Mr. Harper. Giselle sank down low in her seat, face no doubt turning fifty shades of red. All eyes were on her, including Ash and Mr. Puppy-Dog Eyes… staring, laughing. In under thirty minutes she'd managed to make herself a social pariah at this school. *Perfect! Just perfect.*

"Save yourself the trouble and stop trying to talk to me," Asher whispered under his breath.

Giselle counted that a victory in its own little way, but she still kept quiet for the remainder of the class, partially for fear of being called out again by Mr. Harper.

4

Thank God for lunch. Giselle's stomach was so empty it was practically feasting on itself. No doubt everyone around her could hear the gurgling and complaining. Just another embarrassment to add to the list of reasons that home-schooling was a better option for her. She barreled into the cafeteria and headed for the shortest line in the lunchroom. Window-style, like a walk-up fast food joint, there was a menu overhead with generic choices and prices. Giselle ordered one of everything. Pizza, burger, fries, juice, side salad with Italian dressing, the works! She wanted it all. It didn't matter that school lunch wasn't really food. More like foodish-looking products with artificial taste, color, and smell. It didn't matter at that moment. She was starving, and her wolf was restless. She'd gnaw on a table leg if it meant her stomach would stop complaining.

Picking up her overloaded tray, she scanned the room for her group. Feeding time at the zoo would have been easier to manage than school lunch hour. Tables were filling up faster than she could reach them. Pre-determined groups had laid claim to specific areas of the room and set up invisible boundaries that must have been known to the regulars. She certainly couldn't see them, but one step too close to the Goth group earned her sneers and hisses that had her wolf ready to surface. Giselle tried to remember she'd already embarrassed herself more than once today; she'd best be on good behavior at least until day two.

She spotted Di already sitting in the farthest corner near the windows and headed for her. "Where's Taylor?"

Di faux pouted. "She's on second lunch."

"That sucks," Giselle said, and proceeded to stuff her face with a slice of cardboard pizza.

"Nah, she's got friends to keep her company. School council, party planning committee, that kind of thing."

"Overachiever?" Giselle asked.

"Social butterfly," Di answered. "But she's also got the connections. If you need it, she can get it. Pays to have friends in high places."

Giselle couldn't imagine what special things she'd need in school, but smiled and continued to wolf down her food. Onto the sawdust-flavored burger. "So. Who wants to tell me about the other pack here?" she asked between bites.

"Could you be any louder?" Di cringed. "Or more disgusting? Chew with your mouth closed, please!"

She couldn't help herself. That would be the last time she skipped breakfast! "Like anyone listening knows what I really mean." She gulped down a soda and wiped her mouth clean. Vikings probably had better table manners than she at this point, but if she didn't sate the beast, there'd be more problems than sloppy eating. Her wolf demanded more food.

"Whatever, Elle." Di rolled her eyes and scooted her chair a few inches away from Giselle. "Don't stress. The others are not our friends. That's all you need to know right now."

She'd made a big deal about warning her, and that was

her reason? Nope. Not going to fly. "Screw what I need to know. Give me something to work with here. I need details."

Di huffed as if her word were law and to challenge it was an insult. "When you are made an official member of the pack, maybe Martina will tell you. It's not my place."

New family or pack or whatever they were, Giselle could see some arguments in their future. Di's attitude was grating on her nerves, to say the least. But she tried with a cleansing breath to calm her wolf and work a different angle to find answers.

"Fine. If I decide to join, I'll ask Martina. But for now at least tell me about Ash.... The boy. Because I sit next to him in Chem and in Writing. He's..."

"Not. Our. Friend, Elle," Di said with finality.

Giselle grimaced at the way Di tried to shut the door on the conversation. "Maybe not yours. But, as you so poignantly stated... I'm not pack. So I'm not held by those rules yet."

"You will be *pack* soon enough."

"Says who?"

"There's no way you'll reject our pack." Di seemed to think she had the upper hand here.

"Been a lone wolf for a long time, and you're not making this pack sound very appealing," she lied. She very much wanted to be part of a pack, but if denying that would play to her advantage, she had to take it.

Di sighed impatiently. "Geeze, Elle, you just don't give up, do you?"

"Nope."

"Fine," she huffed. "I don't have all the info, but I'll tell you what I do know. He's the youngest of his family. Last one in the pack to finish school here. The whole family has lived here for generations..."

Giselle's attention drifted as Ash came strolling through the cafeteria doors. Head held high, he walked like a man with a purpose, even if he was just joining the lunch line. She caught the flair of his nostrils and the quick flick of his eyes in her direction. Of course he had picked up on her scent, and Di's as well. Two wolves sitting in the corner together would be hard not to smell. Even normal humans should have been able to pick up on something *different*.

As quickly as their eyes met, he looked away and continued on to order his food.

Di snapped her fingers in front of Giselle. "Hey. I'm talking here."

"Oh. Sorry. I—"

"Was ogling the enemy. I know. Wipe the drool off your chin, chica, it's embarrassing."

"Seriously, why is he the enemy? If you won't answer, I will go get the info out of him."

She rolled her eyes. "Why is it so important to you?"

"I'm a lone wolf. I rely on my own wits to keep me safe. That means I need to know everything about my surroundings."

"You're not a lone wolf anymore. You have a pack now."

"Not. Yet."

Her sigh of impatience sounded more like an aggressive growl but the look on Di's face screamed for mercy. "C'mon, Elle. Don't be like this."

She'd get to the bottom of this one way or another; but Giselle wondered exactly how much she'd have to push now that Di was showing her frustration. "Just tell me and we can drop the subject."

"I don't really know, okay? It's like the Hatfield and McCoy crap."

"The what now?"

"Feuding families. The Thrace family and the Hernandez family have both been here a long time. And neither of them wants to leave."

"Why should they? It's not like there isn't enough space for more than one pack to roam the desert."

"That's not the point. Sure, the city can handle more than one pack, but their pack is deliberately trying to shove our pack out."

"Well, a turf war doesn't make someone evil. It's kind of the wolfy way, isn't it? I mean, we're all a bit domineering."

"You are, that's for sure."

"I'll take that as a compliment."

"It's not."

"Afraid I'm too Alpha for you, Di?" She hadn't intended to start a dominance game with Di, but the blonde had just opened the door up for it, and Giselle's wolf was itching to prove she was top dog.

Di's gaze hardened for a moment. Her wolf was rising to the surface as well, and Giselle was ready to meet it, but before anything happened, Di closed her eyes and took a calming breath. "I think you and I will make great sisters."

Not what Giselle had expected her to say, but her words deflated the situation perfectly. Giselle was left speechless. Comebacks she was good at. Compliments… not so much.

"Nice try changing the subject." Giselle was quick to steer the conversation back on track. "You guys act like Ash killed your sister or something."

Di looked down and started picking her nails, chipping away some of the pretty pink polish. "Not Ash, but his father… and it was Martina's sister."

Now things were getting interesting. "Really?"

"That's what I heard. And then paid a witch to curse Martina and make her barren, so there would be no more

Hernandez wolves."

"Wait a minute... Witches are real now, too?" It shouldn't have come as a shock, but Giselle was having issues wrapping her mind around it.

"Seriously? You're a werewolf, questioning the belief in witches?"

"No, I just... Look, up until a month ago I was the only... person of unusual talent I'd ever met. Now I've met wolves from not one but two packs. And you're adding witches to the bunch too. Give me a minute to process, okay?"

"Sure," Di smirked. "Let me know when you're ready to talk about vampires too..."

Giselle's jaw nearly broke it dropped so hard. The whole world was brand new in her eyes. And she was eager to not only learn more but experience it as well. Another quick glance awarded Giselle with a parting view of Asher's hot butt as he walked, lunch in hand, through the cafeteria. Enemy or not, she'd be glad to enjoy the view any day!

"Did I shatter your world view?" Di laughed.

"Expanded it quite nicely." She sighed, eyes still locked by the gravitational pull of his body.

"You're pathetic," Di groaned. "Even if he wasn't the enemy, which he is, you have no chance with Asher Thrace. Just give it up."

"A girl can daydream, can't she?"

"Just don't act on those dreams. He's the enemy!"

"I think the whole feuding families thing is a bit much."

"You would. You're not part of the pack."

"Exactly my point. I'm not. So maybe I'll go talk to Mr. Thrace and see what his side of the story is."

Di laughed. "Good luck there. Martina would forbid it, and she's the pack Alpha."

Giselle glanced over to Ash. He'd just set his tray down

at a table filled with jocks. Through the back patting and congratulations going around, she caught him casting curious glances back her way. She was missing something. Murder and curses. It all sounded a little too farfetched. But if this was what it would be like being part of a pack… she could do without it. Life was stressful enough as it was without adding this kind of drama to the mix.

"I don't like being told what I can and cannot do."

"Part of being pack! Take the good with the bad, and always… always defend your own."

All she had ever wanted was a family of her own. Her place with Martina had been a dream come true. Too perfect. Of course there would be a catch. Giselle glanced over again to Ash. And what a catch.

5

English Lit came after lunch. A subject Giselle was much more comfortable with – and even more so when she spotted Mr. Puppy-Dog Eyes as she entered the room. Seriously, hot guy overload at this school. And despite her earlier faux pas in chemistry, he still gave her a smile when their eyes met. Unlike the taciturn Ash, he seemed almost eager to say hello, and she'd be more than happy to say it back. Aside from the adorable eyes that drew you under their spell, he had a nice body to match. Not very tall, she'd noticed earlier, but taller than she was, which was all that really mattered. And that windswept hair just begged for her to run her fingers through it.

What was wrong with her? Giselle had to stop herself from drooling. She'd never been so boy crazy before. Must have something to do with the moon cycle. As it grew larger, it always played havoc with her moods.

"You have paperwork for me, don't you, dear?" asked an older woman with her hair tied back in a severe bun, with a hand already held out to receive it.

"Yes, here." Giselle fished out her schedule from her notebook and handed it over.

"I'm Ms. Freeman, dear." She spoke with an English accent, which seemed all too appropriate for the subject, and matched her grandma-esque look. "We're in the middle of *Much Ado about Nothing*. You'll need to catch up on the reading if you've never read it."

"I've read it before." She'd hoped to impress her new teacher, but the dismissive look Ms. Freeman gave her said otherwise.

"This semester we are studying the masters, and will be re-creating works in our own pen for the final grade. I'll expect you to hold to the same standard as the others. No leeway for latecomers in my class."

"Will you want it in iambic pentameter, or just in our own words?" Again she tried to show herself in a good light, but it seemed she missed the mark.

"Aren't you just a clever clogs?" Ms. Freeman sighed impatiently. "Have a seat next to Mr. Matthews there in the third row."

Mr. Matthews was far too proper a name for Mr. Puppy-Dog Eyes. Not that her nickname for him was any better, but she'd soon learn his real name, as they'd be sitting together for the rest of the semester. What a stroke of luck. She walked over and took her seat, giving a little hello smile to her new neighbor.

The bell sounded, and Ash strolled in out of breath as if he'd been running the entire lunch break. "Sorry, Ms. Freeman." He threw himself into the seat at the front of the class.

As soon as he'd walked into the classroom, her eyes locked on to him, and she could see a similar response from other girls in the class as well. That boy had animal magnetism to spare.

"Bet you're glad you don't have to sit next to him in this class," Mr. Matthews whispered.

"What?" Giselle said, slightly confused.

"He's a bit rude. Or, at least that's how it looked earlier in Chem."

"Oh. Yeah. That."

"It's okay, I won't bite your head off. I'm not that kind of animal. By the way, I'm Damien."

Why had he chosen those words specifically? 'Not that kind of animal'? Was he some other form of animal? She didn't smell anything other than too much cologne on him, but maybe that was to cover up his natural scent. Could there be more wolves here than she'd originally thought? Was this some kind of supernatural high school? Wouldn't that just be the icing on the cake? Giselle laughed to herself, and then realized that she might have just made Damien think she'd been laughing at him. Couldn't she do anything right?

"Sorry. I'm Giselle."

"You're the new girl, eh?"

"What was your first clue?" She hadn't meant it to come out that way. She'd been going for funny and sarcastic, but it came out as bitch.

"Oh. I see. That's how it is."

"No. Sorry. I didn't…"

"It's cool. I'm crap at small talk too. Let me get your number, and we can have a real conversation."

Damn. Did that just happen? Giselle was dumbfounded, to say the least, but flattered all the same. She bit down on her lip looked away for a moment, hoping the flush in her cheeks might fade before he noticed. Puppy-Dog Eyes… er, Damien… was hot and fast. Probably a bad combination, but what the heck. She scrawled her number out on a piece of paper and passed it over to him. He took it, and a moment later her phone buzzed.

"Now you've got my number," Damien said. "There's a

group heading up to Mount Charleston this weekend. Come with us. You don't have to ski."

Every fiber of her being was screaming, *Yes!* She took a breath and calmed her excitement. "I'll think about it."

"That's girl-speak for no."

"It is not!"

"So you'll go, then?"

"Okay, but I'll have to check with my...friends." She wasn't sure what to call Taylor and Di yet. They weren't really family, and they'd only just recently become friends.

"I'll bet they won't mind. I know Di's going."

He had the self-assurance of an Alpha, that was for sure. Maybe he was one, and all that cologne was masking it. As she wondered silently what she should say next, she caught sight of Asher glancing back at her. Was that disappointment in his eyes? What the hell did he have to be disappointed about? Boys... No point in trying to figure them out.

"How do you know Di?" She tried to ask it with a nice a tone as she could manage, but it still came out as an accusation.

"We go way back. You'll have to ask her, though... nothing bad, I swear."

"You're not exactly earning any points by being mysterious."

"Not something I can talk about in public. If you know what I mean." He lowered his voice. "Wolfgirl..."

She let the words hang in the air, even more curious now about Damien that she'd been before. Clearly he knew about her... and Di.

"I take it you're just as special?"

"Not in the same way, but yes."

Oh, just come out with it already! "Then we'll have a lot to discuss later, huh?"

"So, that means I can call you later?"

She couldn't hide the blush. Her heart had s̲ more than one beat as it raced. Was this really happening. Damn. Hot guy overload and a date. She had to take a breath before speaking again.

"Yeah. Call me."

"And we can talk about the… snow day." Damien sounded a little less self-assured, but only slightly so.

"Right." She laughed under her breath. "If Di's going, I'll have no excuse." Damn. She'd done it again. Why did everything she said have to make her sound like a royal bitch? "Sorry. What I meant was…"

"Books open. No more talking. We're in the fourth act… Giselle Richards, our new student, will you begin to read for us, please."

Giselle smiled awkwardly at Damian. "Mount Charleston sounds like fun," she whispered, and then opened her book up to read.

6

Giselle managed to make it through the rest of the day without embarrassing herself any more. Quite the feat, considering all she normally had to do was open her mouth and embarrassment would just follow.

Walking down the stairs toward the student parking lot, she fumbled through her bag, looking for her phone. She didn't see Ash or his truck until she plowed right into the grill. Thank god it had been parked. So much for not embarrassing herself further.

"Sonofa—"

"Nice. A blind wolf." Ash laughed and walked over to her.

Even if she'd had a witty comeback, at that moment the words would have died on her lips the moment she locked eyes with him. Gorgeous and icy, the most stunning pair of eyes she'd seen, with tiny flecks of blue. Damn, if he wasn't just the perfect package of hot and forbidden fruit at the same time.

"I think you might have a concussion. You have a glazed look in your eyes, and you're drooling."

"Shut up." Embarrassment more than anger colored her

tone. She'd been caught drooling like an idiot in front of wolfboy. *Snap the hell out of it!* She mentally smacked herself back into reality.

"We have got to stop meeting like this," he laughed.

Finally, something other than stony silence from him. If he'd looked hot before… adding a smile amplified it by ten. Damn!

She struggled to her feet but kept tripping over herself. "I've been trying to, but you keep popping up everywhere."

"I was here the whole time, getting into my truck when you ran me over. For the second time today."

"Whatever. I didn't see…"

"The two-ton, cherry-red truck right in front of you."

"Nope." He had her, but she wasn't conceding her last shred of dignity. "Maybe try a brighter color next time."

Ash snorted.

At least laughter was better than the reticent cold shoulder he'd given her all day. "Go ahead, get all the giggles out of your system. And when you're done, you can be a gentleman and help a lady up."

He feigned confusion, looking all directions but hers. "Where? Who? I don't see a lady."

Giselle kicked his shin playfully.

"Oh… you?" Ash asked with a sly grin. "I suppose I could help you this once."

"So you're not planning on making this a regular thing?"

"Not if you're planning on running me and my poor truck down on a daily basis."

"Oh dear. What would people think?"

He extended his hand. "Get up."

"Thanks. My name is Giselle, by the way, since you didn't ask."

"Yep. I know. Mr. Harper… remember?"

"Oh." How could she not? Damn jerkoff teachers loved

to make sure everyone knew your name when publicly humiliating you.

"I'm Ash, though I have a feeling you already know. I saw you sitting with Diana Hernandez."

"You say that like it's a bad thing." The pack animosity was definitely there, though he made a fair attempt at playing it down with a casual shrug of his shoulders.

"You're with them, right? Part of the pack?"

"Not yet."

His eyebrows arched as he cocked his head sideways, a confused look that make him that much more attractive. Seriously… was he a model or something? Every move, every facial expression was GQ-worthy. "You are a wolf. I can smell it on you."

"Lone wolf." Giselle raised her hand as if answering a question in class. "I'm staying with them, but I haven't committed myself."

She wasn't sure of which part of what she said turned him off, but the coldness returned to his eyes and he set his jaw with that stony expression of cold indifference. "If you have a choice… Don't." Asher turned away and walked back to the driver door of his truck.

She should sue for whiplash as fast as he'd blown her off. They'd almost had a moment there, and he'd done a complete 180 back to being an asshole in the time it took for her to blink "That's what you're leaving with?" she mocked his masculine tone. "'Don't'?"

"If you have a choice. Don't join the Hernandez pack. They're not good people. But I think you've already made your mind up, so there's no point in continuing the conversation, lone wolf."

"You say 'lone wolf like' it's a bad thing."

"Just as bad as being part of the Hernandez pack."

Wow. Just wow. Nothing about her was right for this

guy. What a jerk. She shouldn't defend herself to him, but the words flew from her mouth before she could stop them. "Not all of us are blessed with good parents. Or a family at all, for that matter. I don't have a choice on what I am. Hello… foster kid. Not exactly in charge of where I go until I'm eighteen."

Her revelation should have evoked some emotional response from him. You'd have to be one stone-cold jerk to not sympathize with the plight of a kid stuck in the system. But maybe he was beyond comprehending how hard of a life that was, because his reaction just cemented the title of Asshole of the Year for him.

"If you're one of us, and been in the system any length of time, I'm sure you know your situation is not permanent. You can find a way out."

Though his words had some truth, the delivery of them made her want to punch him. Sure, she'd been kicked out of many a good home for being… well, herself. But that didn't make her situation better any time it happened. If anything, each new family, until the Hernandez group, had been worse than the one before. "I am not going to jeopardize my home on the word of a stranger. Especially a jerk like you."

He didn't even flinch at her name calling. Either he was proud of it, or she was so beneath him that he simply didn't care. "You do what you like. I'm just giving you a friendly warning." He hopped up into the cab of his truck and slammed the door closed before she could respond.

Maybe the girls were right. Ash was certainly not giving off the super-friendly vibe, and telling her to screw up the first good home she'd found… not earning any points in her book. If anything, after talking to Asher, she was beginning to put serious thought to accepting Martina's offer.

"There you are!" Di honked the horn on her Prius and waved her over. "Let's go."

Giselle trotted over to the car and hopped in the back seat behind Taylor.

"I saw what you were doing," Di said as Giselle settled next to her in the back seat. "Haven't I already told you? Leave Ash alone."

"No. See, that's the thing. You all are good with the warnings, and not so good with the why."

"Ask Martina. She can tell you what's up."

"Oh, I will."

"But not before we take you shopping." Taylor's cheerful tone helped to lighten the mood.

"What? Why, didn't we just have Christmas?"

"Uh. Yeah. And we have gift cards to burn, and you seriously need some new clothes…. If you're going to be hanging with us," Taylor said as Di gunned it out of the school parking lot.

"You guys do a lot of shopping, don't you?" Giselle snickered.

"Yep. As much of it as I can." Taylor waved a handful of gift cards in the air. "Retail therapy is a good way to pass the time. Besides, Martina called and said she needed the house to herself for a few hours."

"Really? what's she doing?" All manner of devious scenarios ran through Giselle's mind. Asher had been so adamant that Martina was evil, or, her pack was. What if she was up to something? Plotting a pack war? Spying on the other pack? No. Martina was too much the soccer mom type to be involved in inter-pack espionage. Or was that just a really good cover story? Geeze, one word from that asshole Ash had her whole world view compromised. Damn him!

"Don't be nosy," Diana barked at Giselle. "She's probably looking for a little alone time with her husband."

Giselle's mind changed gears faster than a NASCAR driver, and suddenly her super-spy foster mom turned into a stripper. "TMI. Seriously. TMI." She'd need some mental bleach to fix the horrible stains left from those thoughts.

"Well, you asked, Ms. Nosey. Martina said to make ourselves scarce until dinner. So, why not hit the mall and have a little fun, right?" Di wasn't really asking, and the mall was already in view.

Giselle shrugged and relaxed into her seat. Might as well go along for the ride. "Only if I can get some pretzels with cheese from the food court." The school lunch had done nothing for her, and she still felt like eating her weight in junk food.

"Take it easy on the junk food, Elle. You have to learn to control yourself," Di said. "Your metabolism can only handle so much."

"Your inner animal wants meat. Not junk food, but it will settle for whatever it can get. I'll text Martina and see if she has steak available. That should help settle your cravings."

"Thanks, Tay." Giselle had learned something completely new about herself. Shocking.

"See. Good things come from being in a pack. Knowledge is power."

"This afterschool special is brought to you by…."

The girls erupted in laughter as they pulled into the mall parking lot.

7

"With your red hair, Elle, I think we need to steer clear of oranges." Taylor held up a flaming red tank with tribal designs in oranges and browns across the midsection. "But Di could pull this off nicely."

Diana snatched the top from Taylor and held it up to her chest in front of a full length rack mirror. "It's pretty, but I prefer cooler tones." She hung it back on the rack and selected the same top in a different shade.

"See, I wouldn't even know where to begin," Giselle laughed, overwhelmed by the choices.

"Well, lucky you have me here. I'm already Di's personal shopper, so why not add you to my list?" Taylor turned to the rack behind her and found a vintage-looking button-front tunic shirt in heather gray. "This will look amazing. Dress it up with that patterned jacket over there, and finish with some super short jean shorts and a pair of light ballet flats, and you'll have every guy in school wanting your number."

"Every guy except Ash," Di whispered under her breath.

"What was that?" Taylor asked.

Giselle's eyebrow quirked up. Taylor must have been left out of the loop from this afternoon's lunch conversation. "Di was just reminding me again not to speak to Ash."

"With good reason." Taylor continued searching through the racks of clothes, not really paying much attention.

Giselle didn't feel like rehashing everything again, so she let it go. "How about blues? Can I get away with this, you think?" She held up a blue striped maxi dress.

Taylor looked up. "In the spring, yes. Pair it with a white jean jacket and sandals, and go with a nice long silver chain, and you'll look stunning."

"I can see why you're so popular and on all the committees," Giselle laughed.

Taylor flitted from rack to rack like a humming bird in a flower garden, yet her selections were spot on and oh so stylish. Giselle took note of each combination she came up with in the hopes of recreating them later. "I love to make people look good. I suppose that does help me gain friends. It's a win-win."

"You've got a friend in me, then. I need all the help I can get!" Giselle picked up a shirt and held it high.

"Put that back." Taylor barked, shocking her by the sudden change in tone. "You are not falling back on grunge. I won't allow it."

Now it was Di's turn to laugh. "Trust me, you don't want to get on her bad side."

Giselle smiled at the two girls and thought to herself that this must be what it was like to have sisters. That led her down a path she didn't often allow herself to take. Subjects like family – her real family – were taboo. But she did wonder what must have happened to them. If Asher and the Hernandezes were any indication on what wolf families were like, her parents must have been wolf too. At least one of them. She'd like to think she had sisters or brothers somewhere. That maybe she had come from a pack, but something drastic had happened and she'd been sent away for safety. She'd always held onto the hope that she'd find them someday and learn the truth. But, the reality was, she was a lone wolf. Fantasy was one thing, but she didn't have family in the real world.

"Hello! Giselle?" Taylor's face was suddenly two inches in front of hers. "You still with us?"

"Yeah. Sorry. Lost in my own train of thought."

"Sorry if we're boring you – you're just standing there zoned out like an idiot," Di said huffily. "Kind of like earlier today in the cafeteria."

"Yeah. I guess I was daydreaming."

"Tall, dark, and wolfish? Do tell." Taylor giggled.

"Taylor!" Di said, shocked. "You know we don't talk to them."

She didn't need to know who *them* was referring to.

"Who said anything about talking? I just want to look… maybe touch. A little." Taylor sighed.

Giselle was the one to laugh this time. "Only if I can too."

"What is wrong with both of you?" Di sounded mad, but Giselle had the suspicion there was more jealousy there than anything else. She and Taylor had been two peas before Giselle had come into the picture.

"Seriously, though, I wasn't dreaming about the wolf-man." Giselle said. "He's not the only guy in school—"

"Oooh. I like that. I'm going to start calling him that from now on. Hello, Wolfman!" Taylor giggled and Giselle couldn't help but join in, as that had been her first though too when she'd seen Asher.

"Please stop," Di huffed.

"Brat," Taylor said.

"You're one to talk," Di responded in kind.

This was what had been missing all these years – the small things, like arguing with a sibling and shopping. Even when she was younger, in a home that claimed to love her, there had never been anything like this. Di might be a little hard to get along with, but even arguing with her overbearing Alpha-in-training attitude was more fun than Giselle could remember. And Taylor – she was so warm and welcoming. Together, those girls were everything Giselle could want in sisters.

"There she goes again," Di said. "We need to get her head examined. Hey, space cadet!"

"You guys are awesome. Just saying."

"If that's the response I get from picking on you, I'm doing it all the time," Di laughed.

Silently Giselle dared Di to do just that. They'd have lots of fun going round and round. And part of her couldn't wait for the opportunity. But she couldn't find the words to appropriately express it without sounding like a soap opera actress. "Sorry. I just never…"

Taylor threw her arm around Giselle. "Totally understand. Don't let smart ass over here make you feel bad."

"I am not a smart ass." Di crossed her arms in front of her chest.

"Would you like me to use other choice words?" Taylor smirked.

"No. but I do need you to help me find a cute outfit for the Mount Charleston trip."

"Are we really going to that?" Taylor asked. "I don't feel like dealing with snow. I'm ready for spring."

"You can't rush mother nature," Di said.

"Oh, yeah, speaking of that. What do you know about Damien?"

Diana shrugged as if the name meant nothing to her.

"He's part of the local witch coven. Nothing special."

"Okay, because he asked me up to Mount Charleston this weekend too," Giselle said.

"Well, he's a much better choice than Asher, so go. You'll probably have fun." Diana busied herself with looking through a rack of skirts.

"That's it? You lecture me all day long about Asher but shrug your shoulders and tell me to have a good time with Damien?"

"Do you want me to stop you from dating every guy in school?" Di asked.

"Well, no… but it just seems odd that you're so adamant about one."

"Because he's our pack's enemy!" Diana's face turned red with anger. Despite the twitch in her eye, Di said nothing further, though it looked like she had a few more choice words on the subject.

"Whatever." Giselle threw her hands up in surrender. "So. I'm going with Damien. What should I wear?" She directed the question to Taylor, who had hidden herself among sweater dresses.

"Something warm," Taylor said.

"So helpful." Giselle sighed.

Taylor giggled and emerged from the rack, arms filled with clothes. "Why don't you go try a few things on?" She loaded up Giselle's arms and pointed to the back of the store.

"Wear whatever you want," Di said. "As for me, Taylor. Boots are fun and all, but I've had my fill of sweater dresses for the year already. Can you find me something warm and flirty?"

"Of course! You'll be in the lodge drinking hot chocolate with the boys when they've finished their ski runs. So we'll find you something a little more snugly. I wouldn't send you up the mountain in a sweater dress anyway." She hooked an arm around Di and walked her off toward jackets.

The more she time she spent with the girls, the more and more she wanted to make herself a place in this pack. To have sisters and pack mates. To be able to take impromptu shopping trips and ditch class. To have someone to cover for you when you were dating the bad boy... Gods, why couldn't she stop thinking about Asher? Even now when she was having so much fun with her... sisters. But it was more than just simple infatuation. Somewhere in the back of her mind, Asher's warning about the family had taken roots, and the shadow of doubt it caused couldn't be ignored. Why would he say her family was so bad and hers point the finger his way? What was missing from the equation? She'd have to find the answer somehow.

"Giselle, come try this on too," Taylor shouted across the store.

She'd get the answers she needed soon enough, but at that moment, a teal paisley print skirt Taylor was waving in the air was calling her name.

8

Giselle spotted the familiar gray Toyota in the driveway as they pulled up from their shopping trip. Jenny Perkins. And there she was, strolling out of the house, papers in hand, wearing a tight pencil skirt and too-high heels. That woman would never be caught dead in anything less than four inches. How she could manage that Giselle would never know. Some people just lived to torture themselves with fashion. Under the slate-gray peacoat, she no doubt had some trendy top on that paired well with the salmon-colored skirt. She might not have liked her caseworker, but she did appreciate the wardrobe, stylish and always sophisticated. The smile on her face told Giselle that she wasn't in any danger. Unscheduled visits were common in these early days. But with how well things had seemed to be going, Giselle was holding her breath at the sight of potential upheaval.

Jumping out of the car, Giselle jogged over to her caseworker. "Routine inspection?"

The blonde smiled at her with a hint of deviousness. "More than that. But I'm not going to spoil the surprise. Keep playing your cards right, and you might just be rid of me."

"I think we'd both like that."

"Oh. Now don't be like that. You and I go way back."

Jenny lied almost as well as Giselle. She was already mentally celebrating the end of their partnership. It showed so plainly in the excited smile and the way she clutched tightly to the papers in her hand. Adoption papers, if Giselle was right.

"Ink dry yet?" Giselle smirked.

"Don't be such a brat. Go talk to your family."

Giselle noted the intentional emphasis put on that last word, and took it as a sign of good fortune.

Jenny pulled open the door and slid neatly into the leather seat of her car. "Leave me with my papers and I'll get out of everyone's hair."

"Let me know when the celebration begins." Giselle had a lighter step as she walked back towards the house. She'd almost forgotten the warnings and question marks hanging over the family… pack. Whatever she was to call them. Having a place to call home – real home – had shoved aside all the concerns that had been weighing her down on the drive home.

Martina met her at the door looking like she'd been caught with her pants down. "You guys are early. I wanted it to be a surprise."

"I can still act surprised." Giselle let her mind slip into fantasy land where all her dreams had come true. It was so close. So within her grasp, she could almost taste it.

"Well, nothing is official yet. I just submitted the application. It still has to go through all the proper channels, and you have some papers to fill out too, and court dates before anything becomes official, but we'd like to have you here… permanently."

A million thoughts, words, and feelings came rushing at

Giselle, and she could do nothing more than stand dumbfounded as the tidal wave crashed over her. If she opened her mouth surely gibberish would spill out, stringing any coherent sentence together at that point was impossible. She tried to smile but failed at that too, feeling like her face had contorted into something more jester-like than genuine.

"You don't have to say anything." Martina grabbed Giselle and pulled her into a big momma bear hug.

A dam must have burst in her head, because her eyes were suddenly leaking. Giselle couldn't control the flood of tears running down her face. She squeaked out a sound that was meant to be "Thank you," but doubted even the best translator in the world could have understood her. This was all too surreal. Too perfect. How, after all this time, had she gotten so lucky?

"Come now. We're going to celebrate. I had Gavin grab us some steaks."

That roused her from the emotional depths… food. And not just any food… meat! Then it found her – the smell of cooking meat wafted towards her nose and her wolf came rushing to the surface, salivating, ready to devour. If she were a weaker person, she'd have been out there at the grill eating the half raw meat sizzling on the grates. But that would come soon enough. Martina pulled her inside, guiding her towards the kitchen rather than the patio door where her feet wanted to take her.

"This way. I've got more good stuff in here. You've been neglecting your nutrition. Diana called after lunch and told me what you've been eating."

"Damn. News travels fast," Giselle grumbled, and cast a sidelong glance at Di who was just as quickly skipping away up the stairs. "I just had a bit of junk food."

"Language…" Martina had that mothering tone down pat. And the evil eye, too, that made you want to hang your head in shame. But why? It wasn't like she was cursing.

"'Damn' is not a bad word." Her feeble defense didn't have any effect on Momma bear, or wolf, rather.

Martina popped Giselle upside her head. "My house, young lady."

"Ouch! Child abuse!"

"You're no more a child than that was abuse, and you know it. Remember, in this house we are respectful. I do not allow that language, and you will accept that."

So, not everything was peachy in this family, but if that was the worst of it... Giselle snickered to herself. It was nice to have someone to care enough to give you a little walloping for bad language.

Martina rubbed the back of Giselle's head gently. "I know. It's the hunger calling. When the moon is close, your wolf craves more. You need protein and iron. Good healthy meats and nice leafy greens. While the steaks cook, you can help with salad."

Giselle scrunched up her face at the thought of salad. That was the last thing she or her wolf wanted. Green stuff was for the prey to eat! Bloody steak, that was what got her howling.

"Don't give me that face. You need to eat right; otherwise, you'll slow yourself down. Now, we'll have a nice meal and then discuss your welcome home party."

A party? Wasn't that a bit much? "But nothing is official yet, right?" She hadn't meant it to sound the way it did. Years of being shuffled around had made her cautious, and that lingering wonder of what Asher had said still niggled at her thoughts. A month before, she would have never thought this all possible, but now it felt as if things were moving just a little too quickly.

"We'll get it sorted. Don't you worry. We won't let you fall through the cracks. You'll be with us forever. And we can officially welcome you into the pack at the next full moon."

She should have been jumping for joy. Family. Pack. Dreams come true. Family, sure, but for some odd reason her wolf shied away from the idea of being tied to a pack. And Giselle the human too balked at the idea. But those two things weren't a package deal, were they? Could she have a family without pack? What if Asher's warning held some weight, and she tied herself to the wrong pack?

"Child, you look like you're about to be sick. Are you okay?" Martina's calm tone had an effect on her anxiety.

"Just overwhelmed." Giselle wanted to say more, but there were no words to sum up all that was plaguing her thoughts.

"Breathe, honey. All will be well, you'll see."

Martina's calm assurance was almost like a command for her to fall in line. Alpha as she was, Martina's control was a presence in her thoughts quietly urging her, but Giselle's will was strong too. Maybe stronger than Martina's; and being uninitiated into a pack, she could not be swayed by any Alpha's order, even if she wanted to. She had to quiet her own worries herself. Giselle took a breath, remembering what she'd learned from yoga, and tried to focus on the moment, being present in this one space and time. It helped, and so did the warm eyes she found when she looked up at Martina.

"You are all so good to me." Giselle wanted to say so much more at that moment, and to talk with Martina about the questions Asher had raised, but she knew that bringing it up would sour the happiness that the potential adoption should be bringing, and she didn't want to take that risk. Just this once, she wanted to hold on to the fantasy of having a family. A real family. She'd deal with reality soon enough.

9

Giselle couldn't wait to get to Chemistry the next morning. It was the first class she had with Asher, and with fifty minutes next to him with no chance of escape, she was determined to get some information.

Practically flying through the crowds of other kids milling about in the halls, Giselle made quick work of stashing her things in her locker and finding her class.

"They're trying to adopt me." She tried to sound casual as she slid into her seat next to Ash.

Asher snorted, but didn't respond with words. He stared down at the paper in front of him, scribbling away as if copying down notes, but class had not even begun.

Giselle looked over, curious as to what had his attention. On his paper was a beautiful tribal wolf baying at the moon. *Damn, he's a good artist. Must be a tattoo design.* She'd love to have something like that on her lower back, maybe just above her left hip. As Asher continued to deepen the lines on the wolf's tail, Giselle almost forgot what she had wanted to say, but the moment passed quickly.

"Hey, so, did you hear me? I'm getting adopted." She kept her voice low enough that only he should have heard it, and yet he refused to acknowledge her verbally. He snorted again, sort of. At least she thought it was directed at her, but for all Giselle knew he could have just been sniffling from the cold.

"Um… Hello. You heard me, right?"

"Congratulations." His tone said otherwise. Asher continued to stare down at his drawing.

The whole cold shoulder routine was beginning to get on her nerves. If he'd been just another high school prick, she'd have not thought a thing about it; but he was like her, a wolf. That rare condition demanded at least a little attention. "C'mon, after your warning, that's all you're going to say to me?"

"Yep."

"Really?"

He sighed and set down his pen, finally giving her an annoyed but passing glance on his way to grab his chemistry book from his bag on the floor. "I don't know what you want me to say."

"Look. We're the same. The only difference is, I'm still a lone wolf, and your whole standoffish act is really not helping matters. I need to know what's going on."

"Emancipate yourself." He opened the book and flipped through the pages, looking far more interested in the table of elements than he was in the conversation Giselle was trying to have with him.

"I'm in the system… not an option," Giselle whispered.

"Then run away."

"Seriously. That's all you're going to say? I have no recourse here."

"Then I am sorry… for you."

She turned sharply. "What the hell is your deal?"

"Ms. Richards…" Mr. Harper's icy eyes bore down on her with the weight of a Mack truck. He might not have been a wolf, but Giselle still felt an Alpha's presence from him at that moment. Either that, or it was the combination of the weight of all eyes in the room settling on her... again. "Would you like the class to wait while you and Mr. Thrace finish your lovers' quarrel?"

Laughter would have been better than the silent stares Giselle received from the entire class. More frightening was the look on Asher's face. She'd been trying to get him to look at her properly and talk since they'd met, and now all she wanted was his hateful glare pointed anywhere but her face.

"Sorry." She shrank down in her seat.

"If we might begin today's lesson…" Mr. Harper turned back to the white board and wrote an ingredient list. "You'll need to sign out for each of these items before you bring them back to your tables. Notepads are in front of each item with instructions as well."

Giselle turned to Asher. "Seriously. Throw me a bone here."

"Was that supposed to be wolf humor? We're not dogs."

"It got more of a response from you than anything else I've said. Look. If something bad is going on, I need to know before it is too late. I can't do much in my position."

He sighed. "Fine. Open campus for lunch. Meet me at my truck and we'll take a ride. No promises, but I'll tell you what I know."

It wasn't a date or anything like that, but the way he said it made her stomach flutter. She bit down on a smile threatening to break through her tough girl act as she said, "Good," and then scooted out of her seat to head to the front of the class for their experiment supplies.

10

Boys like Asher shouldn't be allowed to have such nice cars. It sent a bad message to girls like Giselle. She'd want to ride around in it all the time, and given her situation, that wasn't likely. It was nothing more than a tease. Not fair!

She came up on Asher leaning against the front grill of his truck, looking damn sexy with that devil-may-care attitude and the deadly combination of icy eyes and dark hair. Seriously, a look like that should be outlawed. The things he could do with just a glance! It made her knees weak just looking at him. And she had the pleasure of spending the next hour-ish with him. Alone. Be still, her heart. It raced as his gaze lifted and those irresistible eyes met hers.

She tried her best to keep cool, while avoiding making a scene by tripping over her own feet. "Where are we heading?" At least she managed to sound calm and collected.

Asher crossed his arms, looking as if he were planting himself in the spot. "I didn't say we were going anywhere."

"It's lunch. I'm starving. Aren't you? Full moon is coming soon."

He shrugged. "I have control over my hunger."

Of course he does. They all do. "Well, I don't. I didn't grow up with wolves. Never got the nutrition lessons."

Slowly, almost lazily, his eyes traveled the length of her body. Not in the way she'd hoped, though. Judgmental. If a simple glance could be such; but disconcerting all the same. She might not have been rich, or even from a real family, but she was worth his time. Maybe she was reading too much into it. With the full moon's pull so strong, she was likely reading things with too much emotion thrown in. Still, though, the silence between them was unnerving.

When he finally spoke, she'd almost forgotten the conversation, lost in her own insecurity.

"You need meat."

"Funny how everyone keeps saying that."

"It's a fact, and one I can see you're in desperate need of. You're weak."

"I am not!"

"Let me guess. You're emotional, defensive, and probably exhausted right now, correct?"

A little, but she was always this way around that time of the month. Giselle shrugged.

"Too much crap food. Not enough rest, and definitely lacking in red meat… lots of it!"

"Whatever. I'm more than just a carnivore."

"You could be vegan for all anyone cares, but the wolf is a predator and a carnivore, so deal with it."

To hear him talk like that was odd. He should be on the junk food bandwagon with the rest of the highschoolers. But Taylor and Di had said similar things. Maybe it really was a wolf thing, and she'd never had someone to teach her the importance. "I'll deal with my carnivorous nature when you hop in that truck and take me to a burger place."

Asher laughed, genuinely, for what was probably the first – and maybe the last – time. When he wasn't being a jerkoff, he was really damn cute. Especially with that super wide smile that revealed all his teeth. If she hadn't known he was wolf, she might have thought him a vampire for the sharpness of his canines.

"You've got some Alpha in you, has anyone ever told you?" His tone might have been playful, but there was a serious edge to the question.

"Yeah, Martina."

"That's why she wants you." He scoffed and jumped into the truck. "Get in."

She didn't need to be told twice. Her stomach grumbling for food and she was eager to hear what he had to say, so she was in the truck and buckling her seat belt in seconds. "Okay. Tell me what you know. What's the deal with the family feud?"

"Bad blood between the families."

"Obviously."

"And lies. And rumors." He started the truck and drove slowly out of the student parking lot.

"Again… Thank you, Captain Obvious. Details!"

"We wolves are a proud bunch… born wolves, not turned wolves. Wolf families are huge and close-knit, even in packs that spread across state lines. Multiples are common for wolf moms too; did you know that?" He didn't give her a chance to answer. "My family has two sets of twins, then me."

That might put her off sex forever. Pregnancy was a scare most girls didn't want to have, but multiples while still in school… or any time, for that matter, were way too much to handle. "Okay, and where are we going with this lesson on family planning?"

"Martina has no kids of her own. Don't you find that odd?"

"I hadn't until you just mentioned it."

"She's barren, and she blames my father."

"Did your dad do something to her?"

"No!"

"So then why would she blame him?"

"Martina had a sister. She and her sister were a twin set."

Giselle's eyebrow lifted at that new piece of information.

"Back in the day, the packs here were working to align through marriage. Martina's sister was promised to my father."

"Okay, so how many packs are here in Vegas?"

"Two now, but there used to be another. Moved down to Phoenix, last I heard."

"Okay, so two packs joining together in wedded bliss."

He scoffed. "Not exactly. Before the marriage, it was found that the sister, Christina, had been having a secret relationship and was already carrying the other guy's child."

"Okay." Giselle shrugged. Nothing shocking there. "Arranged marriages don't work these days anyway."

"Wolf packs are different. You do as your Alpha says, no questions asked. She defied her Alpha and betrayed our pack."

"Can't blame her."

He tightened his grip on the steering wheel. "Yes, you can. Pack law."

Giselle scoffed. *Pack law. Bunch of bull!* "Good reason to stay a lone wolf then."

"Don't laugh at things you don't understand." His tone bordered dangerously on anger.

She'd touched a nerve with her comments, obviously. These things seemed so silly. Arranged marriages in this day. Who would expect any of that rubbish to work? Still, she noted his annoyance and the way he sped down the street, and decided it was better to ease up on her attitude.

"Sorry, go on. So she defied the pack."

"Yes, and insulted my family. My father, obviously, refused the marriage. It didn't go over well with either pack."

"Okay, so, where's Christina now?"

"She died... unfortunately."

Giselle had a pretty good guess how that happened. Made sense now why the two packs hated each other. "How?"

Asher shrugged. "No one really knows, but my father was blamed."

"Well, obviously."

Asher slammed the brakes, nearly sending Giselle through the windshield. "He didn't do it!"

"Sorry, that was petty of me to make assumptions." Giselle quickly backpedaled. "So that started the hatred?"

"That, and the rumor he hired a witch to curse her family so they would never have children to continue the pack line."

"Did he?"

"No." Asher shrugged.

"That doesn't sound convincing."

"Well, my father had nothing to do with that. But I wouldn't put much past my grandfather where revenge is concerned. He'd been more disappointed about the ordeal than my dad had. And Martina being unable to have children despite the adoring husband she has is also quite odd."

Very. But Giselle had only known the husband and wife team for roughly a month. Maybe they were just lovey dovey for show. "Okay, so the two packs have hated each other since the botched marriage."

"That's putting it mildly. A small war broke out, and wolves from both packs were killed. Right now we're in sort of a cold war standoff. Neither of us are making a move, but that doesn't mean we're not ready to battle again. And every bad thing that happens between our families makes it worse. Like my cousin going missing during the last full moon…"

"And you blame Martina for that?"

"He was running in her territory."

"So. Was. I."

He arched an eyebrow at her. "The entire time?"

"Most of it. I had to wait to be sure the coast was clear before I snuck out."

"Well, eyes are on Martina. It's not the first time she's killed a trespasser in her territory."

"I just don't see that happening. She'd never kill." No way. Martina was too sweet for that.

Asher smiled wickedly, revealing his teeth on purpose as he spoke. "You're so sure? And how long have you known her? We're all predators." The way he said that sent a delicious chill down Giselle's spine. That guy was the full package. Sex on a stick. So damn yummy, and yet, so distant and unreachable. She had to make sure she savored this little car ride together; chances were it would be the last they could share. If she signed on to be in Martina's pack, she was as good as his enemy.

"So what's the Alpha part of the equation?"

"She's building her pack selectively instead of through birth. My pack are all born wolves, and we all fit together in our roles: Alpha, beta, and omega. Like a pack should be. She's stacking the deck, and we think she's preparing for war. No pack should have such an imbalance of power."

"I think you might be over-thinking things. She can't choose who she gets through foster care. Besides, have your two families ever attempted to talk peacefully?"

"No. Only the Alpha deals with another Alpha."

"Well, then have your Alpha talk to mine. Stop this

bullshit."

"The bullshit has not even started. Stay away. My Alpha will get to the bottom of my cousin's disappearance and punish the pack responsible."

"Was that a veiled threat?"

"Take it as you like. But when we find out for certain it was Martina's pack, retribution will be swift. You do not want to be part of that."

"Oh so you're warning me, then..."

"We're here." He pulled the car into the parking lot of Grinder's Burgers. "Get your food and I'll take you back to school."

Despite her desire to argue with him some more, the call of freshly grilled beef wafting on the breeze had her wolf's full attention. "We're not done here."

"Yes, we are. Get your food and heed my warning. I can't say anything more."

Giselle slipped out of the truck and headed inside. She'd get to the bottom of things, and soon – before she lost her new family, one way or the other...

11

Lunch had been nice, even if she'd forced herself into Ash's company. When he wasn't being a standoffish prick, he actually had a sense of humor, and there was a hint of some personality too. But she'd heard the warnings from her family, and he'd echoed the same sentiment. Too bad the families had to be at war, pointless as she found it to be.

Giselle walked to her locker alone, thankful not to have her overbearing escort yapping in her ear. No doubt as soon as she found out Giselle had taken lunch with Asher, she'd get an earful and a reminder to stay away… as if she cared.

"You want me to pick you up, or are you riding with Taylor and Diana this weekend?" Damien surprised her, appearing almost out of thin air behind her. And that was saying something – with her wolfish hearing, usually nothing got past her.

Giselle took a second to calm herself and then shut her locker and turned to face him. They met almost nose to nose. Definitely not a tall boy, but the perfect height for kissing. She blushed and he smiled, as if in on her little secret thought. "I'll ride with them and meet you at the lodge."

For the briefest of moments his smile faltered. "You

sure? We'd have plenty of time to talk on the drive."

As much as she'd love to ride with Mr. Puppy-Dog Eyes, she felt it best to stick with the girls, at least until she got to know him a little better. But damn if she wasn't tempted! Especially when he was standing there all cute and sweet, eyes begging her to say yes. She needed to change gears. "You act like you're just itching to tell me something."

He shrugged, a casual movement, but one that just added to his appeal. He had that perfect combination of sweet and confident down pat. "Just nice to find another kindred spirit. There are so few of us around here. And with you being new and all, we'd have more to learn about each other."

"Seems quite the opposite to me. I've never met so many... special people in such close proximity before."

"Your family and the Thrace family are special, that's for sure. My people are not so rare, but there aren't any others here at school. My coven draws from all across the valley. "

A hundred questions popped up the minute he said 'coven.' She could quiz him for hours on what it was like to be a witch. Her only ideas about magical people came from fiction, and as she'd never seen him raise a wand, she was fairly certain her imagination was probably a bit far from the real thing.

"Well if it's any consolation, Di gave you the thumbs up. So, you're on the approved boy list." It sounded so much better in her head, but when the words left her lips she found herself speaking like a schoolmarm rather than the interested flirt she wanted to be.

"Well, that was kind of her." Damien looked confused for a moment, but that did not steal the smile from his gorgeous eyes.

Trying to recover from the awkwardness, she giggled and said, "She's protective…"

"You mean she told you to stay away from Ash, and I'm a better choice by comparison."

"Mind reader much?" The fact he knew that was off-putting, to say the least. She was really beginning to feel like a newb. All the supernaturals seemed to be in on all the secrets, and she was nowhere near up to speed.

"I've lived here a long time. I know the two packs aren't friendly, and I saw you taking off at lunch with Ash. I know your sisters wouldn't approve."

"They're not my sisters…"

"Yet."

She thought to correct him, but decided to change the subject instead. "So you're keeping tabs on me, then?"

"Whoa." He held out his hands and backed away a step as if waiting for her to strike at him. "Don't make me sound like a stalker. I was in the parking lot heading to lunch when I saw you hop into his car."

A likely story, she though. Actually, she was still wondering if all the supernaturals were having secret meetings or at the very least texting one another without her. "And what do you think of him?"

Damien shrugged. "He's a wolf. Not much else to say."

"I'm a wolf." Somehow that sounded more normal than anything else she'd said to him the entire conversation.

"Yes, but you're a pretty wolf." Those sweet eyes locked on to her and he winked. "And Ash is not really my type."

Giselle couldn't hide the blush rising to her cheeks. She could easily fall for a guy like him. He certainly said all the right things, and with those eyes… well, witch or not, he had her under a spell. So much so that she was tripping over her own tongue trying to find ways to continue the conversation. "I…So…Where did you go for lunch?"

"Home. I live around the corner. Maybe I'll show you sometime."

"I wonder how many girls you've made that offer to." She wasn't sure where she was going with the conversation, but she liked talking to him. He felt easy, like an open book. The complete opposite of everyone else she'd run into. Ash, Taylor, and Di all seemed to have pack-related agendas, but Damien was free of that. And maybe because he was interested in her, he was more willing to chat. Or maybe he was just that kind of guy. Either way, even though she had nothing else to say, she scrambled for something, anything, to keep the conversation going. "Or am I special...because of the full moon?" That totally didn't come out the way she'd planned. Could she sound like any more of an idiot?

"Yeah." He laughed. "You're special. But not like the others."

The hint of uncertainty in his words made her question his true meaning, and she looked at him quizzically.

"That's a good thing, Giselle. I like you. Tay and Di are pack animals. I sense something different from you, and I'd like to get to know you better."

"Not much to know, but you're welcome to try."

"I like a challenge." Those puppy-dog eyes melted through her defenses. God, she could stare at them for hours. She wondered if that was a witchy thing. Asher had animal magnetism, that was for sure; maybe Damien had the same, but a witch version? Damn. Why did Ash have to invade her thoughts when she was standing here with Damien? She gave herself a mental slap and fell back under the spell of Damien's eyes.

"You're smooth. I'll give you that."

He gave her a lopsided grin, and held out a hand to help her with her bag. "You want smooth? You ain't seen nothing yet."

Giselle giggled as Damien grabbed her bag and books and hooked an arm around her to escort her to class.

12

Giselle raced out to the parking lot, searching for Diana and Taylor. The day had been one of discovery, and she needed to find her sisters, or friends, or whatever they were to find out what else she might be missing. They weren't hard to spot, parked right next to Ash's truck. Too bad the wolfboy wasn't there as well. She could use a good show. Lunch had been such a treat – but the finality of the way it ended told her the most she could expect from that point on was a little eye candy every now and again.

Diana honked and waved Giselle over, and she threw herself into the car as soon as she got there. "No bullshit, girls." Giselle said squeezing into the seat behind Taylor. "Truth time."

"Well, now, that's no way to talk to us," Di said.

"I'm going to level with you. Martina has not only asked me to join the pack, but she wants to adopt me."

"That's wonderful," Taylor shrieked. "We'll be sisters for real!"

As nice as it sounded, she still had things niggling at the back of her mind that needed clearing up. "It's not all roses…"

"Um, yes, it is!" Di's tone went beyond sharp. "You've got a family now. Isn't that the dream of any foster kid?" She'd been frustrated with Giselle's unwillingness to follow orders to stay away from Ash, and it was beginning to show.

"It's too quick, too rushed, and Ash said…"

"Oh. Yeah. Him. Don't think I didn't catch you sneaking away to lunch with him today."

"You did what?" Taylor sounded more shocked than angry. "Not him!"

Diana narrowed her eyes in the rear view mirror at Giselle. "Asher has been filling your head with bullshit, I'll bet." Anger amped up the volume of Diana's voice, and Giselle's wolf rose to attention. "His pack hates ours, Elle. Bottom line: don't listen."

"He makes some valid points, and I'm coming to you all for reassurance before I make any judgments." Giselle did not let her annoyance color her words yet, but if they kept blocking her, it would.

"Fine. Like what?" Di huffed. Her tone had mellowed, but if the way she pulled out of the school parking lot was any indication, she still had plenty of pent up rage to exorcise.

Giselle tightened the buckle of her seat belt. "OK, for starters… did you run into any other wolves on the night you all met me?"

"No. I don't remember anyone," Taylor said. "Well, except you. I honestly didn't know if we would. Di and I had a bet going…"

"Wait. No," Di interrupted. "There was some older lone wolf running in the desert. He didn't stop or get in our way. Just kind of ran off." She continued after a pause. "It's happened once or twice before. As long as they don't stop, Martina lets it slide."

"Did you know Ash's cousin went missing that night?"

Giselle asked.

"Oh, and let me guess, we got the blame?" Di was quick to defend. A little too quick, in Giselle's opinion. Speed like that usually meant guilt, at least as far as Giselle was concerned. Her wolf agreed as well, but she kept her tone neutral.

"Yes, actually. Ash did say that the pack was possibly responsible."

"Well, we didn't do anything." Her defensiveness was a bit too overplayed. "He blew past us and ran away. Case closed."

"You sure about that?" Giselle asked, unconvinced.

Taylor shrugged. "I really didn't see."

"Yeah." Di sounded terribly annoyed, and she was channeling her frustration into speeding around corners and almost blowing through a stop sign. "There was no fight, no killing. Might as well have been a rabbit for all the attention we paid it."

"Did you actually see the wolf run away, or did Martina chase it off?" Giselle asked.

"You don't sound like you're on our side anymore, Elle." Di pulled the car over and turned to meet Giselle's eyes with a menacing glare.

Giselle could see the wolf below the surface of Di's eyes, just itching for a fight – and hers was equally ready. "I'm simply asking questions. Interpret them as you like."

"Take it easy, Di," Taylor cut in before the argument escalated. "She's curious. And understandably so." She turned on Giselle. "There was no fight. No killings. The biggest thing that happened to us that night was finding you in wolf form. Honestly, we weren't even sure you were a wolf at that point."

Giselle took a minute to calm her wolf. Di might have been on the defensive, but Taylor was speaking the truth.

There was no threat in her words, and Taylor's wolf was at rest, no sign of it in her eyes. She didn't want to fight with the girls, and hadn't intended to get riled up, but the way Di jumped to anger at everything she said and did really worked her nerves and tested her control. "Okay, was that so hard to tell me?"

Di huffed.

"She's new to the family. And with the bad blood between our packs, it's understandable that things might get ...murky." Taylor was clearly the voice of reason, so Giselle directed her attention to her.

"I'm just clearing the air. The fact that there is a potentially hostile pack around makes me worry about setting down roots," Giselle said, as calmly as she could.

"You don't have a choice, really. You're a foster kid." Di smirked, and Giselle felt a strong urge to smack her in the face.

"So were all of you, right? How did Martina manage to collect a perfect set of kids for her pack?" That question had been niggling at the back of Giselle's mind since her earlier conversation with Ash.

"Dunno." Taylor shrugged. "I was adopted as a baby."

"And you?" Giselle directed to Dianna.

"Two years ago. I came from Florida."

"And you don't find it odd at all that every foster kid she's taken in and subsequently adopted has been wolf?"

"Maybe there's a supernatural agency," Taylor joked.

"There would have to be. Three kids, that's not dumb luck."

"So what are you getting at?" Di put the car back in gear and started driving down the road.

"Something Ash said..."

"Him again." Di threw her hands up.

"Yeah, because he's the only other wolf I can talk to.

Deal with it," Giselle snapped.

"What did he say?" Taylor asked.

"That Martina may be stacking the deck in preparation for war." Giselle sighed.

"Look, our two families hate each other, but war... no." Taylor shook her head.

"You said their cousin went missing?" Di spoke up.

"Yeah, same night I arrived." Giselle answered.

"Coincidence?" she asked.

"I doubt the two are connected. But what is important is that Martina and Gavin are to blame... according to Ash."

"They didn't do it. I swear," Taylor said.

"Then we'll have to find a way to prove innocence," Giselle said.

"Wait. Why do we have to prove anything?" Di asked.

"Because if Ash's dad is under the impression our family is preparing for war, and one if his has gone missing, presumably killed by our family... Hello? Self-fulfilling prophecy."

"You assume way too much." Di flicked her hand.

"Here's the thing. I'm sick of being bounced from house to house. I'd actually like a home. So, if there is any chance in making this one work, I'm all for it. But I won't hang around for a war."

"Do what you want, Elle. Run away. Keep being a loner," Di said.

"Di, shut up. She's saying she doesn't want that. And you know what... I'm not really keen on being in a war either. If what she says is right, we should get to the bottom of this. Help prove Martina's good and maybe we can all get along."

"Tay, when did you become all kumbaya?" Di shot back at her.

Taylor shrugged. "You know I don't like to get my claws dirty."

Giselle snorted. "I'm not saying we go all Nancy Drew, but we can look into it. Take a run. Sniff some things out."

"And what about your initiation?" Di glared at Giselle through the rearview mirror. "Full moon will be here before you know it."

Giselle shrugged. "I don't have to decide now. I'm used to being a loner. I'll wait it out."

Taylor didn't look too pleased to hear that. In fact, she looked on the edge of tears, but was holding them back. "Martina is not going to be happy about that."

"But she'll respect my decision," Giselle said.

"You sure about that?" Di sounded like she hoped the answer would be no and that she could have front row tickets to see the fallout.

Giselle had had just about enough of Diana's attitude. "If she's as good as her word, yes. I'm still very new to this family. And I've never had a pack. This is a bigger decision than you think."

"We made the decision. And we are all happy with it," Di said.

"Yes, but you two were adopted before you had made your first shift."

"True… but how can you live with us if you aren't pack?" Taylor looked genuinely confused.

"Just as I am now, I guess. I'd still have to follow house rules, but I wouldn't be bound by pack law."

"I still say she'd not going to go for it," Di huffed.

"Leave that to me. I'll deal with the fallout."

"Fine. When do you want to take a run?"

Di's sudden change of subject had Giselle doing a double-take. "Ummm. Why not tonight? Seems as good a time as any."

"After dinner then… and after you break the news to Martina." Diana glared at Giselle through the rearview mirror.

"Really? I have to tell her tonight?"

"Yeah. Rip that bandaid off quickly," Di said.

Giselle rolled her eyes. "Fine."

13

Giselle knew what she needed to say, but the uncertainty of Martina's response had her close to trembling as she sought out her would-be mother. Martina had been busy preparing dinner. That woman was a chef! Wolf or not, you could smell her tamales from half a block away, and by the time you reached the front door, you were practically drooling. Maybe she should start with a compliment. Smooth things over before telling her the truth. If stalling were an Olympic event, she'd have the gold for sure. Giselle wasted as much time as humanly possible as she warred with herself while she paced around the living room. There was just no good way to start this kind of conversation. She'd rather say she was failing algebra or maybe even pregnant than tell Martina she just wasn't ready to join the family... just yet.

Damn Diana for forcing her hand so quickly.

"Dinner's not ready yet," Martina called out from the kitchen.

Damn. She'd been spotted. Now or never.

"Give me another half hour, okay?" Martina hadn't even looked up as she said it, but that didn't matter. Her presence had been noted.

Giselle gave herself a mental kick to get moving. *Just do*

it and get it over with. "Martina, can I talk to you?" Rip the bandaid off, as Di had counseled.

Martina looked so hopeful as she walked out from the kitchen. "Something the matter?"

"I need more time." Giselle had wanted to go with tact but ended up just blurting it out.

Martina's reaction surprised her. Rather than anger or sadness, as Giselle expected, Martina's brow creased with bewilderment. "Why, dear?"

Heart racing, Giselle had almost forgotten her reasons. Martina looked so confused; and if she was being honest with herself, Giselle was the most confused of the pack. And she wasn't even in the pack. She hated to disappoint, and even more than that, she didn't want to screw up her only chance at a home, especially after all this time. "This. It's just all… so… overwhelming."

No anger. Not even hurt. Martina was the picture of calm. "Take a breath, hon. You look like you're going to faint."

"No. I need to say it before I burst. This is all wonderful, but too much too fast." She hoped she was conveying her message well enough. "More than I ever hoped for, and at the same time, so much more than I was prepared to handle."

Martina reached out and pulled Giselle to her chest. "Aww, sweetheart. It's okay. I hadn't thought about coming on so strong. I just wanted us all to be family."

She stroked Giselle's hair, and Giselle's heart ached for the mother she'd never had. This had to be what it was like. The comfort. The warmth of loving arms surrounding her. Martina was such a comforting presence. How could she possibly be part of a pack war? Only cold-blooded killers were involved in wars, right? That damn niggle in the back of her mind could not let her give in. It demanded the truth before she could accept this home for what it could be... her forever home. Her family. Oh god, how she wanted a family to call her own!

Despite the war raging within her, between head and heart, she snuggled closer to Martina. Every stroke of her hand in Giselle's hair was heaven. Listening to the steady and calming beat of Martina's heart was a siren's call home. Her home. Maybe...

She would get to the bottom of it all. She had to. Giselle would have a mother and father and sisters to call her own. She just had to make sure the offer stayed on the table just a bit longer.

"Martina, you're wonderful, and everyone is so wonderful here. I just... I need time to process it all. Before I tie myself in. You know I've always been a lone wolf. The whole pack thing. It's so much more than family, and I've never even had a family, so everything is just..." She rambled on like an idiot, hoping Martina would give her time.

"Don't even think about it, sweetheart. One step at a time for us. After the next full moon, maybe you'll be ready to make a decision. Okay?"

"Yes." Giselle smiled and breathed a sigh. That was exactly how she'd hoped it would go. Thank the gods. She pulled back and met Martina's eyes, finding just as much relief there as she felt. "Thank you."

"No thanks needed, sweetheart." Martina stroked her hair once more, her face serene as ever. Did anything ever rile that wolf up? Giselle wondered. "We've all been loners at some point. Family can be quite an intimidating transition."

"More than you can possibly imagine," Giselle said.

"Oh, I can definitely imagine." Martina let out a little laugh. "Now, go tell the girls that dinner will be on in half an hour."

Flooded with relief, Giselle raced up stairs skipping them two at a time. Mission accomplished! She had the time she needed; now all she had to do was clear Martina and Gavin's names, and she could have the family she'd always wanted. Simple, right? She laughed at her own joke as she walked through the bedroom door.

The girls were lying across Taylor's bed reading magazines and giggling over the quizzes inside.

"How'd it go?" Di looked up from her quiz on relationship compatibility. "Are we sending you back to the orphanage?"

"Funny," Giselle smirked. "Yes, the sun will come out tomorrow for me."

"Aww." She faux-pouted. "But you do have the red hair for it. Maybe I'll just start calling you Annie anyway."

"Why? You're not getting rid of me just yet. I'm good, at least until the next full moon."

"Well, at least Martina knows the truth, that you're not fully invested..." Di turned her attention back to the quiz.

Giselle chose not to rise to the taunting of her would-be sister. There was probably a very good reason for Diana's defensiveness. Maybe she was just being a good little wolf and protecting her own. Yeah. That had to be it. Because if it wasn't, and Di was just being a bitch, she'd make sure to show that girl her place at the first chance to pull her wolf out.

"So, what's the plan for tonight?" Taylor asked, breaking the suddenly awkward silence in the room.

Giselle hadn't really made any plans. Aside from getting out after Martina and Gavin had said good night, she hadn't had a chance to think things through. She didn't know what to look for either. Just any sign or clue that there were other wolves about.

"Taylor, want to stay behind and keep a look out?" Di ordered more than asked.

"Why do I always have to be the one to stay?" she huffed.

"Because you're Miss Goodie Two Shoes," Di answered.

"No. I'm not staying. You stay."

"Whatever, Taylor."

"Nope. Don't look at me. I'm going."

"We can't all go. What happens if Martina comes upstairs?" Di asked.

"Then you tell her a few creative lies. That's something you're exceptionally good at." Taylor stuck her tongue out.

"How about you both stay and I'll just go. Seriously. The bickering…" Giselle was beginning to get a headache, listening to them argue.

"Fine, I'll stay." Taylor sighed. "If only to shut Di up. But don't be long, okay?"

14

Gavin peeked into the girls' room. Giselle could smell him coming up the stairs and had even caught sight of his large frame in the door way before he pushed it open all the way. "Night, girls. Don't stay up too late." He waited as Taylor and Di both came to give him a hug good night before turning away and closing the door.

"Give it about two minutes, and you should be good to go." Taylor flopped back down on her bed and resumed dog-earing pages in her magazine with cute outfits, trying a little too hard, in Giselle's opinion, to hide her feelings about being left behind.

"Thanks again, Tay." Giselle gave her a nod and understanding smile. "Promise I'll take you next time."

"So, you're planning on making sneaking out a habit, are you?" Di's accusation bothered Giselle more than she wanted to let on at the moment.

She couldn't read that girl. Was she trying to be a good sister? Was she trying to ensure Giselle got caught doing bad things? Was this the downside of having family?

But there was no time to worry about that – they had other things to do. Giselle opened the window and slid out onto the pergola, padded to the edge, and hopped down. "Be on the lookout for us, so you can come let us back in later," she whispered up to Taylor.

Di followed quickly behind, and as soon as they were at the back gate, they stripped down and shifted.

Just beyond the edge of the alleyway, the neighborhood exited out into open undeveloped desert as far as the eye could see.

Nothing felt quite as good as running top speed through that open desert. Giselle could see why Martina had set down roots in this neighborhood. The freedom of wind rushing through your fur and plenty of open space to enjoy was the best feeling in the world. No stress. No worries. Just the wide open space to put distance between you and all the cares in the world. Every time she shifted and allowed the wolf to the surface, she felt that blessed freedom and wished she could live it permanently. Life as the wolf was uncomplicated and carefree. Her wolf, a lone wolf by birth, only needed food, shelter, and freedom. The trappings of social norms and packs seemed too much to bother dealing with. If she truly had the choice, she'd stay with the family but not tie herself down to a pack. But of course, that was not a feasible choice, though it would save her all this trouble. Just the freedom and open desert. Yes, that would be enough for her. Was that a jackrabbit? She picked up the scent and quickly darted off in another direction, completely abandoning her mission as her wolf took over. Hopping again through brush grass and dodging cactus, she gave chase after the little furball, determined this time to catch it.

She'd run for a good twenty minutes before Di's nipping at her legs pulled her back to reality. Miles from home, they'd hit an area Giselle had never been in before. All thoughts about catching her prey evaporated as the sudden realization that she could have gotten herself lost sank in. The mountains made a natural border for their territory, preventing them from going too much further, or so Giselle had initially thought. But she wasn't sure now how far she'd gone from the housing development. She could hardly tell which neighborhood's lights she was seeing in the distance, and hoped if she couldn't, that Di would still be able to get them back home after this little adventure.

Di looked to her, but Giselle couldn't tell if it was in anger for her detour or if she was waiting for directions of some kind. That was one downside to wolf form: no verbal communication. She could convey general messages like *run* and *stop* and *retreat*, but the finer points of conversation were lost in barks and yips.

She tossed her head and listened for a moment, catching the sound of water, and trotted off in that direction. Di followed close behind.

A small stream ran into the mouth of a very tiny cave, one she'd just be able to fit through in her wolf form. Intuition told her not to investigate, but curiosity got the better of her, and she snuck inside for a quick peek.

Dark. Way too dark without the moon and stars to help her see. And cramped, too. Something large and rock-like took up almost all the space inside; but with no light, she couldn't quite tell what it was. Venturing farther into the cave seemed ill-advised, even assuming there was space farther back. Other than a place to hide out from the elements, it really didn't seem too exciting. But Giselle made note of that in case the need ever arose. A little disappointed but no worse for giving it a go, she left the cave and found Di on alert just outside. Di was looking around strangely, sniffing the air, ears twitching this way and that. Something was up.

Di's ears pinned back and fur began to rise on her back.

Giselle went on alert as well. She looked around, smelling
the air for any strangeness, but came up short. Whatever it
was, she wasn't picking up on it. Too many other smells to
sift through: rabbits, coyotes, wet earth, dust, and a few
other foul things she'd rather not think of.

Di took the lead now, slowly padding back the way they
had run. It was then that she caught it: just a faint wisp on
the air, but enough for Giselle to pick the scent. Musky,
dark, and definitely masculine. More than just the wet dirt
smell, there was someone else. Another wolf nearby. A
werewolf, like them.

Following Di's lead, Giselle retreated slowly at first, but
a snap of jaws behind them had her jumping into a gait.
Running as fast as her paws could carry her, then, she
almost overtook Di in the lead, but the speedy wolf was not
going to fall behind. Giselle couldn't help herself. She cast
the briefest of glances back behind her, not able to see
much beyond the dirt her paws were kicking up, but she did
catch the glint of icy eyes. One more quick glance back for a
better view earned her the sight of sharp fangs nipping at
her tail.

That was close, too close. The sting of hair being ripped
away as the wolf tore out a chunk of her tail was enough to
spur her on faster. She bit back the yelp but used the pain to
push her paws faster than before. She followed Di's lead
again, wondering where they were headed. The desert all
began to look the same as they zigged and zagged, rounding
short and tall cactus plants and bounding over rocks. She
kept running. Though they were quick, the wolf giving
chase was having no trouble keeping up. Even when they
scrambled over a rough patch of mountain rock and slid
down into a small valley, they found their pursuer close
behind.

Fearing they'd soon run out of steam and be overtaken

by the wolf, Giselle entertained the idea of turning and making a stand. Two wolves were better than one, right? When she'd drummed up the courage and put on the breaks to turn around, she found the other wolf had suddenly disappeared.

The girls looked around, not wanting to move for fear of being pounced on from above. They waited in silence, listening to all the desert sounds. Nothing. Even the breeze had no hint of the other wolf. How and why he had disappeared was a mystery, but one they would have to figure out another time. A quick look up in the sky told them they had spent enough time. The moon was high and clear, being nearly full. They'd only meant to be out for an hour at best, but the chase and subsequent waiting had taken them well beyond that. They needed to get back, fast. Taylor was good with distraction, but only for so long. The downside to wolf parents was they were practically able to smell a lie.

With a flick of her tail, Di signaled to head out, and they both bolted back toward the house as fast as their paws could take them.

15

She was never happier to see Taylor at the back gate waiting for them. She let them in and ushered them through the sliding glass door and up into the bedroom without alerting Martina and Gavin. Or, at least, they hoped that was the case. Either way, as soon as Giselle was safely inside the bedroom, she shifted and turned on Di. "Who was that?"

Diana looked equally clueless, but no less shaken than Giselle. "No clue. Never smelled them before."

Taylor was eager to get in on the action, "You found someone? Spill it!"

Giselle picked up her pj's and pulled on the pants. "Yeah, we found someone all right. Someone new." She tossed her shirt over her head and pulled it down. "That could be good news?" she said, hoping the newcomer could take blame for the cousin's disappearance.

Diana didn't look so convinced. "Or really bad news. That was in our territory." She pulled her clothes on as well, nearly ripping her shirt with the speed she was dressing. "Granted, just on the edge of our territory, but in our normal run area."

"Maybe it was the cousin that went missing? We should

have tried to talk."

"Um, hello! He was going to kill us."

"We might have spooked him?" Giselle was grasping for a feasible reason, but knew deep down that running had been their only real option. Two young girls against a feral wolf; odds were not in their favor."

"That kind of thinking gets lone wolves killed. He could have had backup nearby. He could have had a whole pack. You don't approach a strange wolf unless you have your pack ready."

"Okay, so next time we all go." She hadn't really meant it, but didn't want to give Di the benefit of having the last word.

"Or maybe we mention this to Martina. Look. It's one thing to say we want to go find clues. It's an entire other to find a stranger waiting in our back yard." Di's domineering tone had returned.

"You're over-reacting. That wasn't our back yard."

"Close enough, damn to it!" Di said. "We're warning Martina."

"And how do we explain why we were out?"

"Easy. I tell them you wanted to run away, and we stopped you."

Giselle's jaw dropped. Dumbstruck, she wasn't sure how to respond. Di was clearly throwing her under the bus, but for a cover up story. A damn good one too, if it worked. But she'd be in deep trouble.

"Fine. I'll take the heat."

Di screwed up her face. "Wait. What?"

"Do it," Giselle said.

Di eyed her curiously as if wondering whether she should call Giselle's bluff or not. After a silent few moments between them, she shouted, "Martina!" and then took off down the hallway, heading for the stairs.

"Didn't actually think she'd do it." Giselle tossed a wayward glance at Taylor.

"You don't know Di very well," Taylor laughed. "Best get down there. Who knows what story she's spinning."

The girls tore down the stairs and found a very angry looking Martina there to greet them in the kitchen.

"Giselle…" Martina said, clearly disappointed. She stood eerily still, in her bathrobe and slippers, looking as if Di had not only thrown her under the bus but woken Martina from a sound sleep in the process. No one every handled news well when they first woke up. Giselle needed something, anything, to appeal to Martina's mothering side, and quick.

"Before you start, I know. I should have talked with you more about what was going on. But let's save the lecture for later. We have bigger issues to deal with."

"You think you're getting out of this easy, huh?" Martina's hands on her hips and crazy eyes said more than her words about just how much trouble she was in. "You just wait until I tell Gavin about this. We're all going to have a family meeting about this in the morning. And you can bet our full moon festivities are canceled."

That had the girls collectively groaning in disappointment. Now it wasn't just Martina but the girls who were angry at Giselle. She wanted to explain her reasons… her need to go out and search for clues, but talking about it would only distort the facts. Which she really didn't have – only hearsay between the two families. Stupid fighting. Just pointless. And all she'd wanted was a damn family to call her own. Part of her, a small part, wished she'd never met Asher. If he hadn't said anything, she'd have happily gone along with becoming a pack member. But no. He had to go burst her bubble with pack politics. Maybe he was right all along. Maybe she should just run away. She'd been a lone wolf all this time. Might as well make it a lifestyle. Anything was better than the deadly glares she was getting from everyone in the small kitchen.

"Is no one concerned about the lone wolf that attacked us?" Giselle asked.

"Wait one second. You met another wolf?" Martina's anger ebbed, but just slightly.

"Met, not so much. Chased by. Hunted down. Near mauled by… take your pick. He meant business."

Martina pulled Giselle into an unexpected bear hug. "You. Don't you ever run off like that again!"

"Not the reaction I was expecting."

"Just happy you're alive. All of you." She pulled the other girls into the hug, and Giselle thought she might faint from the air being squeezed from her lungs. "You don't go running without me. You hear?"

"We were in our own territory," Di said.

"Doesn't matter. You're pups."

"Hey!" Taylor said in mock annoyance.

Martina let them all go. "You are. Until you're of age and married off, you're pups, and you can be picked off by lone wolves." She shot a wary eye at Giselle. "Lone wolves don't respect boundaries. Or rules. Even Thrace wouldn't attack a pup, and he's despicable."

"So, you knew there were lone wolves around? How long have they been out there?" Giselle asked.

"Honey, that's the nature of a lone wolf. They come, they go. Who knows how long they've been there?"

"But you'd know if they were killing off pack members, or other wolves, right?" Giselle asked.

"Why are you so curious?"

"Well…" She wasn't sure where to begin or how much she could get away with saying. "I would assume. If there was a lone wolf out there, you'd want to clear them off quickly… since they pose a risk for us. Unless maybe they were dangerous, and you were afraid of them."

"Have you heard something?" Martina asked, and there was no mistaking the order in her voice.

Giselle shrugged casually. "Just that another pack has a missing wolf."

"Talking to the Thrace boy, eh?" Martina looked unimpressed, and her hands returned to her hips with disappointment. "Rumor-mongers. The whole lot of them. Don't you listen to a word that boy says."

"That's just it," Giselle said. "He's not spreading a rumor. He was concerned for his missing pack member."

"Sure he was. And I'll bet he said it was my doing?"

Giselle paused, not wanting to tell the truth, but not really knowing how to answer without giving away all she really knew. Martina looked ready to run out and murder the whole lot of Thrace wolves if she got the wrong message. Giselle's voice waivered. "Uh…no. He just asked if I'd seen anything strange. Was concerned for everyone."

"Concerned?" Martina snorted. "That'll be the day."

"No blame… really."

"So you get the bright idea to go out there alone and look for a lone wolf yourself? Dragging my girls into the danger with you? What were you thinking?"

Her girls? Funny how Giselle was suddenly excluded from the family now that she'd shown part of her hand. "Sorry. Stupid idea. I thought…" Giselle fidgeted on the spot, wringing her hands and looking sadly at the ground. "Maybe I would find another loner, like me. You know. Someone who doesn't have family." She might have overplayed it a bit, but she saw her words strike a chord with Martina. The anger faded just slightly from her eyes, replaced with something resembling… guilt, maybe.

"You have a family, if you choose one. You know that.

We offered that to you."

"And I'm still wrapping my head around it. I guess that's why I wanted to find the lone wolf. Maybe see why they chose to remain that way. I knew it was a long shot, but I had to try. Everything is so confusing." Even the girls looked like they were buying it. Watery eyes all around the room, everyone focused on Giselle as she gave her sob story cover up.

"Confusion is no excuse for putting yourself in danger. Do you hear me?"

"Yes, Martina. I'm sorry."

Another bear hug confirmed she was out of trouble for the moment. And the thumbs up from Taylor behind Martina's back was almost as good as a standing ovation for her performance.

"Listen. Yes, from time to time there is a loner out there. We deal with them when we have to. Don't go running at night without myself or Gavin, and you'll be fine. But, even with that in mind, I don't want you going out again without telling me. No sneaking around. We're more than family here. We're pack, and I'm your Alpha. Understand? Giselle, you too… unofficial or not."

"Yes, Martina," the girls answered back in unison.

"Good. Now get to bed before you wake Gavin and get another earful!"

16

"I can't believe she bought that story!" Di flounced on the bed with a huff.

"If I didn't know any better, I'd say you wanted me to be in trouble, or maybe even get kicked out of here." Giselle wasn't putting up with any more bullshit. She stalked up to Di, looking her straight in the eyes. "Thought we were family."

Di rose up to meet Giselle's silent challenge. "You're the one that doesn't want to be here."

"Never said that."

"You're out searching for reasons *not* to be here."

"Look. I'm not getting into this again with you. If we've got a problem here, then let's settle it like wolves, because I'm not putting up with backstabbing from anyone."

"Tough words… loner."

Giselle snarled, her wolf rising to the surface, itching for a fight.

"Stop it. Both of you." Taylor tried to step in between the girls, but only enough to get their attention. Di was already sprouting fur and Giselle was baring her teeth, ready for the kill. "This is not the way we do things, and you know it."

"Back off, Tay," Di ordered.

"No. You'll have to fight me too, then." Taylor's threat sounded more like a plea, but still she held her ground.

"You don't have to defend me," Giselle growled. "I've been taking care of myself for years now. You think this is the only pampered princess I've put in her place?"

"That's what you think of me?" Di's hateful tone faltered, and confusion took the place of the anger in her eyes.

Giselle was still ready for the fight. "Yeah, Gucci Bag… I do. You've had it easy. You've had family, pack, and money. I've been tossed from bad house to worse house, and had to fend for myself. You're giving me shit because things are too good to be true here and I'm worried? No. Not cool. I'll be damned if I am going to take that crap from some Prada-wearing princess."

Shock rather than anger washed over Di's face. She relaxed and allowed her shoulders to slump. Her fur faded as she stopped the transition and let out a sigh. "I guess… I didn't really think of that. Sorry. Look. I'm just trying to protect my family here. We're close, all of us. I may be a pampered princess, as you say, in comparison to you – but I love my family. I love Martina and Gavin, and I don't want to see you hurt them."

Giselle really hoped that was the case, rather than the alternative – that her would-be sister was out to get her. She took a deep breath and let it out through her mouth, back to her yoga breathing. Bringing her focus to the present allowed her to send the wolf down to rest, for the moment. When she'd relaxed herself, she sat down on her bed and found a calm voice to speak with. "I'm not trying to hurt them. Don't you see? I want this family. I do. But, I also have to make sure it's right. Clear out the question marks that Ash brought up, so I know I'm making the right choice."

"You lone wolves... strange breed." Di shook her but there was a smile hiding at the corner of her mouth.

"Yeah... whatever. Can we stop being bitches now?"

Taylor laughed, and the whole room seemed to brightened. "Thank God. I really thought I was going to have to break the two of you up."

"Nah. You'd have had to let us fight it out and watch Martina charge in here and give us a lesson on who the real Alpha is."

"So, do we call a truce for now?" Di looked at Giselle, but this time, there was no hidden anger. She was genuinely curious.

"I guess."

"But you're still thinking of going back out there, aren't you?" Diana huffed. Annoyance was still there, but Giselle could see her actively trying to rein it in.

"I don't know what to do, but I won't do anything rash until I clear it with you both, okay?"

"Not the answer I was hoping for, but... whatever." Diana rolled over and hit the light switch.

"Well, whatever you're going to do... has to wait until later. I've got an early class tomorrow and I am not missing my beauty rest," Taylor said, as if that were the deciding factor in all of this.

Giselle stared up at the bunk above her wondering what she could do. How was she going to find out more of this loner? At least she had something to tell Ash. Her family might be exonerated. With a loner in the forest, that meant their missing cousin might not have been accosted by Martina. Part of her problem was already solved... at least, she hoped.

17

The mood the next morning was less than optimal. Martina's sentence of no full moon fun had soured things, and a less than restful night of sleep hadn't helped either. The girls said hardly a word to each other as they got ready for school. Giselle was more than happy when they all went their separate ways after pulling into the school parking lot.

She took her time walking through the cars, hoping to maybe catch sight of Ash or even Damien. The latter at least would be happy to see her, but the former would be able to provide some more info.

When she spotted the red truck pulling in, she quickly checked to make sure her would-be sisters weren't around to get mad at her and ran up to Ash's truck as soon as he killed the engine.

"So." She hardly let him get out before bombarding him.

"So, what?" He sounded annoyed and looked even less happy to talk to her than usual.

That put a damper on her plans. She'd hoped to wow him with what she'd learned. Now she'd settle for at least passing interest. "What can you tell me about the lone wolves prowling the desert?"

He shouldered his backpack and closed the door of his truck. "That's what you're annoying me with this morning?"

Why did she bother talking to him? Her shoulders slumped and she turned to walk away.

"Sorry. I didn't mean that." For once, Ash sounded almost sorry, but that wasn't enough for her to turn around and continue the conversation. She'd written him off as a jerk once and for all when he blurted out, "There are none that I know of. My father and your foster mother are diligent in keeping the stragglers away. That, at least, is one thing they both agree on."

Interesting. Seemed this time she knew something he didn't. Giselle turned around against her better judgment and gave him her best taunting glare. "What if I told you there *was* a loner?"

That got his attention. His whole demeanor shifted, and if she wasn't mistaken, he looked almost eager. "Where?"

"Open desert out behind our neighborhood. There's a cave in the foothills of the mountain."

"How did you find him?" His eyes lit with more than just excitement. If she didn't know better, she'd have thought he was anxious to go find the loner himself. But did that mean she was right, and this new information could exonerate her foster mom?

"He found me and Di last night. We… were having a run." She probably shouldn't have sounded so cocky. The moment the words left her lips, she realized how bad it sounded – two wolves alone in the desert.

"Alone?" And now it seemed like Asher was going to echo the earful she'd gotten from Martina on the subject. Not a lecture she wanted to revisit.

"Yeah."

"Stupid."

She couldn't argue – he was right – but she slapped his arm in mock anger. "Thanks."

"You never go running alone."

"I wasn't. I was with Di." As if that made a difference; but she wasn't letting another person, a pup, lecture her.

A growl rumbled up his chest.

"Oh, no! Don't go getting all Alpha male on me here."

"Two young... female wolves. Alone in the desert. Are you seriously defending your actions?"

"Men." Giselle sighed. His intentions were good, but the whole caveman approach he was taking was off-putting.

"Yes. Men... do bad things to little girls."

"What? Where the hell did that come from? And who's a little girl?"

He stepped in close – too close. His massive frame dwarfed hers. In human form, he was formidable; she could only imagine his wolf form. "I'm just saying... not smart. For any pup."

Point made... for the moment. She was small in stature and at a disadvantage alone against a full-grown male. "I get it. Whatever. Can we stay on topic, though? Do you want to hear about the lone wolf, or are you going to lecture me some more on the hazards of being a girl?"

"Tell me where he is, and I'll go have a look for myself."

"You're not going out there without me."

"You're not going anywhere near a lone wolf again." If it weren't for the male chauvinist pig in his voice, she might have appreciated the attempt at keeping her safe.

"Well, you're not going onto my family's territory without permission."

His eyebrow arched curiously. "So, they're your family now?"

"Maybe soon." She shrugged.

"You're not going to tell me where the loner is, are you?"

"Nope. But I'll show you."

He sighed, conceding defeat, and walked around his truck to open the passenger door. His sudden gentlemanly action caught her off guard. "Fine. I tried. Let's go." His words, however, ruined the gesture.

"Wait, what? Now?"

"Don't tell me a big brave wolf like you is scared to ditch class."

Who knew he could be a bad boy? She kind of liked the combination of forbidden fruit and deviant streak. "Are you teasing me, Thrace?"

His expression was still stony, but the hint of mischief in his eyes said otherwise. "Maybe."

"Let's go, then." Giselle hopped into his truck and buckled herself in.

As he pulled out of the parking lot, Giselle caught sight of Taylor, standing by the main entrance, shaking her head and staring right at them as they drove off. Giselle sighed, knowing she'd have some explaining to do later.

18

We shouldn't be doing this. The thought ran through her mind over and over as they drove, but Giselle couldn't bring herself to say it aloud. Her wolf was anxious too; she could feel it, ready to surface and at the same time uncertain whether or not it should. At least this time, if she met the lone wolf, she'd have another at her side capable of fighting.

"Where did you last see him?" Ash's sharp tone snapped her from her thoughts.

"Park here, and we'll run towards the foot of the mountain. We'll be looking for a small creek that marks the boundaries."

He pulled the car over to the side of the road. To the left was a beautifully landscaped neighborhood filled with modern two- and three-story homes. To the right, bare open desert waiting to be developed and yet, still untouched. It went on for miles, with only the mountains to stop it.

The sight of all that wide open space to run had Giselle's wolf ready. She hardly even considered the embarrassment of stripping down in front of Ash before doing it, though as modestly as she could. Giselle wandered around the back of the truck, slipped off her jeans and shirt, tossed them in the truck, and immediately called her wolf up.

Tingling from the sudden shift and feeling the gentle breeze through her fur, she took off at a trot, reacquainting herself with her paws before glancing back to see that Ash had done the same.

Her wolf was gray and black with white paws; Ash was completely the opposite, solid black with not a speck of color anywhere. He appeared massive, with a lion's mane of hair around his neck and a long tail. He stood a full head higher than she as well. At that moment, she felt very glad to have him on her side, but dared not show her apprehension at his stature for fear of him trying to impose dominance. She might be an Alpha in her own right, but by his sheer size, he would crush her in a fight.

The two came nose to nose as Asher sniffed her. She was tempted to do the same. Her wolf was curious and, if the situation were different, she might have allowed it, but they were here for reasons other than getting to know each other.

Asher, though, continued his inspection of her. Touching felt wrong, even if it was the wolf way. She'd been a loner for too long and didn't want to partake. She nipped at him and turned away, taking off at a run toward their destination.

Giselle didn't bother to look back; she knew Asher would be close behind.

Oh, how she loved the feeling of the soft dirt under her paws. The way she sank in ever so slightly with each press against the earth, and the little bit of dust that her paws kicked up behind her. Twisting through cactus and hopping over tufts of bushy grass, this was more fun than sitting in a classroom. Especially when she'd have been in chemistry at that moment, where Mr. Harper had it in for her.

Asher caught her and ran alongside, darting through the desert obstacles as easily as Giselle and with just as much enjoyment. Asher nipped at Giselle's tail and darted off to the left. She growled playfully and gave chase, catching up quickly, and returned with a nip of her own at his heels before putting on a little speed and dashing ahead. The two continued their game of tag all the way to the creek, where Giselle came to a sudden stop. There it was, at the end of the small bubbling stream: the foot of the mountain with the cave she'd seen the previous night. This was the spot where the wolf had found her and Di. And, Giselle would have bet that the cave was his den.

She sniffed the air and ground, hunting for any signs of the other wolf – a bit of fur, a paw print, a scent trail to where he might have run off to. She hunted for any clue, but this was unfamiliar territory. Making sense of the smells around was difficult as there were so many to choose from. And the cloying dirt that had given wolves away in the past was too easily covered by the water running alongside them. No wonder he'd picked this as his spot.

She knew one thing – the cave had to be important. The lone wolf wouldn't have been so protective if it wasn't important, so that was the direction she needed to take. Giselle yipped at Asher and took off through the water toward the mountain. No more time for playing.

Asher followed. She slowed her pace and took her time weaving around rocks, following through patches of Joshua trees and over bulbous barrel cactuses, hoping to catch a sign of the other wolf. But there was no sign of anyone around now. She stopped at the cave entrance and gave a quick nod to Asher, and then sniffed at the air, hoping to pick up some trace of his scent.

Asher too sent his snout upward before looking back toward Giselle.

Luck wasn't on her side. No trace. No smell. Not even a recognizable footprint was there at the spot. She decided to sniff around a bit more before entering the cave, just to be sure. No point in risking surprise when they were in no big hurry.

Nothing.

It was now or never. If the cave were the lone wolf's den, she'd be risking everything going inside, but with no sign, no trace, not even a footprint to warn her away, the cave was the last place they should check.

She didn't have a good way to communicate this to Ash. This was something that would need more than a tail flick or a waggle of her ears to properly convey. So Giselle did the best she could – yipped and tossed her head toward the cave.

Asher snorted and sat on his hind legs. Was that his way of saying no? She tossed her head again and pointed her snout at the cave.

Asher shook his.

Well, fine, I'll do it myself, Giselle thought, and took a step toward the cave.

Asher growled and took a nip of her tail.

She growled as she turned to face him, baring her teeth in warning.

He must have understood then, and in his typical male way, he brushed past her and squeezed into the cave ahead of her.

Men!

She ducked inside after him. There was not much room, especially when his massive frame filled the space, but there was also something else inside. She scooted in as best she could and allowed the light from outside to shine in.

She'd half-expected to see a wolf; what she hadn't expected was for the wolf to be made of stone.

Now she was well and truly confused.

Asher looked equally uncertain. They both stood still, shocked at the sight of a perfectly carved and what must have been hand-painted female wolf. Gray and white, with snowy paws and tail. She was beautiful. But what the hell was she doing out here in the desert? And in a cave, of all places?

When the moment of awe had faded, Asher pushed his way outside the cave again.

Giselle took a few extra minutes, still wondering of the origins of the statue. Was it some piece from the Strip that had been stolen and taken here as a joke? She'd heard of people and things being taken to the desert, but this was a whole new level of weird.

Stepping out into the bright sun again, she found that Asher had shifted.

Holy hell, that boy was hot! And the full frontal view was beyond words. She'd seen images of naked men before, but this was the real deal. Mr. *Au Naturel!* Giselle was never more relieved for the mask her wolf form provided because at that moment she'd have been fifty shades of red in her human form. She hardly registered that her tongue was lolling out of her mouth as she stared at him.

Asher didn't looked bothered in the slightest to be naked in front of Giselle. What he did look, however, was annoyed. "So, we wasted the entire morning for what? A stone statue? Is that your lone wolf?"

Giselle had to shake herself from the stupor, still gawking at the naked hottie in front of her.

"Is this a game to you? I've seen you staring at me. Was this your plan to get me out here alone for yourself?"

Truth be told, yeah, she'd been more than happy to have alone time with him, but before she could shift and get the words out, he turned on his heel, growled, and started to walk away.

Giselle whimpered. At a loss as to what to do.

"Should have known better than to trust you."

That was it. She shifted as quickly as she could and shouted, "Ash. Wait!"

He turned around, and the anger softened as he found her standing naked.

She did her best, crossing her legs and using her arms, to cover her breast and hair, but she wasn't fooling anyone: naked was naked. And he was a boy. But at least for that moment, he wasn't glaring at her angrily.

"This wasn't a trick. I really did see someone last night."

"Then why is there no trace?"

"I don't know, okay? I just don't. I can't catch the scent, I can't spot tracks. I'm sure this is where we were." She was almost in tears between the embarrassment of being naked and the fact he wasn't believing her.

"All animals leave behind traces of some kind. If there are none, then there was no one here."

"But I'm sure this is where we were! The cave…"

"Give it up. I'm tired of this game. If your loner was out here, he's long gone." All the softness he'd had a moment before left, and she caught the anger flaring up again in his eyes. Even if that weren't the case, the tone of his voice said clearly that he didn't believe her. He might have earlier, but definitely not now.

"Let's head back to the truck."

Giselle shifted back to her wolf, feeling so thankful for her fur coat. She put her nose to the ground and kept searching. There had to be something. Ash was right: all animals did leave traces. He couldn't have hidden his.

"C'mon, Giselle. I don't want to leave you out here in the desert."

She ignored him and kept going.

"Fine," he growled. "I tried. You can walk home."

Giselle turned in time to see Asher shifting back into his wolf form, and as soon as he took shape, he trotted away.

Well, she'd blown her chances with him, that was for sure. And the lone wolf was still nowhere to be found. How the hell was that even possible? She was certain she had been here the night before. She sniffed around a bit more before giving up in frustration and turning toward home. But, as she looked across the horizon, panic seized her chest. She wasn't sure which was home was. Everything looked the same in the desert. And since she'd run round and round in circles trying to find the other wolf's scent, there was no telling where her true trail outward was. She let the panic settle for a moment and decided to concentrate on finding Ash's scent. He had recently left, so his trail should be fresh and easy to follow. It took a few minutes. Giselle doubled back and sent herself in the direction of the mountains, and finally after a bit of wandering, she found his scent. Damn, he even smelled good, too. Why did there have to be such tension between them? Finally, she'd found a family and it was everything she wanted. Too bad the fine print included a family feud with the hot werewolf boy's father. Why was she so damn fixated on him anyway? He was just a boy. A very cute boy. A very, very cute werewolf boy. Gah. Life was just not fair.

At least she'd found the trail, and the creek. Things were beginning to look up. She took a quick splash as she crossed the water of the creek and stopped just on the other side to get her bearings.

Funny how the desert can turn you around. You think you're heading in the right direction, and then suddenly you're miles out of the way. She spotted a glint of light in the distance – Ash's truck probably. As fast as he ran, she had no doubt he was already there, starting it up and heading back to what remained of

the school day. She'd have to come up with an excuse.
Taylor had seen her, and that meant she'd need to be ready
with answers as soon as she got back to school.

And then she remembered her clothes were in Ash's
truck.

Damn it! She'd have to make a quick trip home before
heading to school. What a crappy day this was turning out
to be.

Giselle was so lost in thought she'd no chance to pick
up the scent of the predator right behind her. He was on
her in seconds, teeth biting into the scruff of her neck. She
yelped, more from the shock than the pain, though that
quickly followed, and tried to roll and knock the offending
wolf from her back. She could try all she wanted, but he was
big and bulky, like a lead weight pushing her to the ground.
Knife-sharp teeth ripped through her skin, even through the
thick tufts of fur protecting her neck. Giselle squirmed and
again tried to roll to either side, hoping to get some traction.
The wolf on her growled and jerked his head, taking a
chunk of fur with him as he ripped it from her flesh.

She yelped again, but this time was able to roll away
without his teeth pinning her to the ground. She squirmed
from under his body and stood, blood trickling down her
neck. All instincts told her to run and she did, taking off at
full speed, not chancing a look back.

The other wolf was right at her heels -- she could feel
the break of dirt behind her paws. He was practically upon
her, and the snap of his jaws were so near her tail he might
as well have been flossing his teeth with her fur.

Focusing on the distance, she saw the light glinting off
of Asher's truck. If she could just make it there, even if he
was gone, she'd be okay. Her neighborhood lay just over
the wall, and no wolf, not even a loner, would dare show
himself to potential human watchers. At least... she hoped

so.

With that thought she added to her own luck by letting out a loud howl, hoping that alone might deter her attacker.

In the moment she slowed to she let out her call for help, the other wolf was on her again, tackling her to the ground. This time, his teeth didn't find the wounded scruff at her neck. His sharp canines latched on to her throat as he pinned her down.

She'd wanted to see this lone wolf. Hoped to find him. And now that might prove to be the last thing she did. His angry eyes bore into hers, molten lava with blind hatred. The larger wolf was black, just like Asher, but with one major difference: he was graying around the eyes, like a small mask to hide his identity.

She whimpered, the effort alone painful with his teeth so deep into her neck. If she could shift and use her words, she would beg for her life, but Giselle doubted that would do her much good.

She closed her eyes, waiting for the final blow, but the other wolf did not take it. He eased back and sat on his haunches.

She squirmed up back to her feet as fast as she could, ready to make a break for it or to fight, whatever she needed to do. Every instinct told her to run, but a tiny voice wondered why he'd spared her.

For a few silent moments the two eyed each other, neither making a move to attack or shift. Now that she was getting a better look, she could see that the graying hair of the other wolf covered more than just his face. He'd been solid black like Asher in his youth, perhaps, but he was no young kid now.

Giselle let out a sigh and sat down behind a rock. Sending her wolf back, she shifted forms. A huge gamble on her part, and one she hoped would pay out better than bringing

Asher here.

Awkward with her lack of clothes to cover up with, she kept most of her body behind the large rock to avoid letting the stranger see anything more than her head and shoulders. "You spared me. Why?"

An answer would have been ideal. But the other wolf still sat silently, staring in her direction.

"Who are you?"

The lack of response was beginning to grate on her nerves.

Finally, after what felt like an endless awkward silence, the wolf shifted and sat down. Grisly old loner that he was, he certainly looked the part, down to his sunburned skin and matted hair. Giselle wondered if she'd seen him before, begging for money near the freeway onramps.

"You're not part of either pack, are you?"

An odd way to start the conversation, but at least it was an answer.

"Nope. Loner. Just like you."

"You're hardly like me, pup."

"Well, I don't belong to any one family. I think we have at least that much in common."

"I don't belong to either of these two families, no."

"So, what are you doing out here?"

"I should ask you the same. And why with the Thrace boy?"

She shrugged, not wanting to give him the truth – that they'd been looking for him "We had a date in the desert."

"Hardly, or he wouldn't have left you alone… Coward."

"How long were you spying on me?"

"I could ask you the same."

This was infuriating. "Who are you, and why are you here?"

"Sweetheart, go back wherever you came from. Leave

my business alone, and I will forgive you trespassing on my land."

"This isn't your land. It belongs to Martina."

"I thought you didn't belong to any pack."

"I don't… yet."

"Well, despite what Martina says, this is my land. When you cross that creek, you are in my territory, and I have every right to kill trespassers. You wouldn't be the first, and you won't be the last if you don't listen up. Let that be your only warning."

"What's so special about the desert beyond the creek?"

"None of your business, pup."

"Does it have something to do with that wolf statue in the cave?"

He snarled. "Leave my territory alone. I don't like to kill pups, but I will if you bother me again."

"That statue is important, isn't it?"

The old wolf shifted and snapped his jaws at her.

Giselle hopped backwards and on instinct, called forth her wolf and shifted down too. She crouched low, slowly backing away, keeping the old wolf in her eye line.

Another snap of his jaws, a warning, and the old wolf turned and ran back towards the creek.

It wasn't exactly how she'd hoped things would work out, but at least she'd made it out alive. She waited until the old wolf was out of sight before turning and heading home.

19

Taylor had been waiting for her the moment she showed up at the house. How the hell had she known Giselle would come back here was a mystery, but she was so happy to see her would-be sister at the gate. Giselle shifted at the back gate and walked inside, trying to avoid the accusatory gaze.

"You going to explain why you ran off with Ash? And where are your clothes?"

"Nope. No point."

"You had sex with him, didn't you?"

That stopped Giselle in her tracks. "No way. Not even close. Why would you think that?"

"C'mon. We've all seen how hard you've been crushing on him. You've wanted to jump him since the moment you laid eyes on him."

"Okay, first of all, um… no. He's cute, sure, but I'm not jumping on anyone."

"Right."

Giselle turned her back on Taylor, letting the marks on her neck show. "I found the wolf."

"Elle, Oh. My. God! Are you okay? C'mon, let's get you inside and clean that up. Does it hurt?"

The speed at which she changed gears had Giselle doing a double take. She'd gone all Mother Hen and was channeling Martina so much, Giselle wondered if Martina might have been right there guiding her. "I'm fine. Really. Most of it healed with the shift."

"If you call this healing, that wolf must have done one hell of a number on you. There are at least four separate bite marks here. He didn't try anything, did he?"

"Who, the loner? No. But he was odd."

"You talked to him?"

"He's defending that spot for some reason – the cave at the edge of the creek. And I think it's tied to a statue I found out there."

Taylor pulled her into the bathroom and began rubbing her down with alcohol and slathering creams on her. "Should completely heal with the next shift."

"Thanks."

Taylor wrapped her arms around Giselle and gave her a quick squeeze. "Glad you're okay." Then she smacked Giselle on the arm twice. "And that's for going out there without backup."

"I had Asher."

"And I noticed he wasn't with you when you got home. Did the bastard bail on you when the wolf showed up?"

"Before. We searched for hours and couldn't find him. So Ash gave up. Pretty pissed for me sending him on a wild goose chase."

"Angry or not, that's no excuse leaving you out there all alone. See, those Thrace wolves are assholes."

At that moment, Giselle agreed. If Ash hadn't been such a hot head, he'd have stayed long enough to see the wolf, and maybe help protect her. Boys! Who needed them?

"Yeah, he's an ass. I'm over it." She lied more to herself than to Taylor. "Do me a favor…"

"What?" Taylor eyed her suspiciously.

"Don't tell Di... please."

Taylor narrowed her gaze. "How are you going to explain missing school at the same time as Ash? She's bound to have noticed."

Giselle shrugged. "How am I supposed to know his schedule? I was having a sick day."

The look on Taylor's face said more than words how bad a lie that was, but she simply shrugged. "Whatever."

"I owe you."

"Yes. You. Do."

Giselle worried about what the ramifications of those words would be. But her sick excuse was becoming more real by the moment. Maybe it was adrenaline, maybe it was the bite the wolf had given her, or maybe she was just coming down with something. In any case, she needed to lie down.

"Thanks," she said, and headed up stairs to her room. "I'm going to skip the rest of the day too. I need to sleep."

20

"Hey, asshole!" Taylor shouted across the quad at Asher. Giselle ducked behind her sister, trying to avoid being seen. Asher briefly looked over and just as quickly turned his head in the other direction. He continued walking with a purpose, as though her attempt at embarrassment had no effect. But the speed of his pace said otherwise. "You shouldn't have left her to get hurt," Taylor shouted again, but it was no use. He either didn't hear her or didn't care. Probably the latter, since wolf hearing was exceptional.

Ash might not have responded to Taylor's taunting words, but she had the attention of the other students within earshot, who were gawking, whispering, and finger pointing. And Giselle felt even stupider now for crouching and hiding behind Taylor. Lord only knew what rumors were being started.

"Why did you say that?" Giselle grumbled in a whisper, standing up and pretending to adjust her shoulder bag.

Taylor's anger hadn't subsided as she turned on her sister. "Those bites wouldn't have been there if he'd been there to protect you."

True. They should have healed by now, and Giselle

wondered why, even after another shift, they were still raw and itchy, possibly becoming infected. She was too scared to look, but even with a scarf covering her neck, she was sure the redness was showing through. If this kept up, she'd be forced to go to Martina and tell her what happened. "I'm sure it will be fine. Wolf bites must take longer to heal, is all."

"Well, still. Pissed off or not, a gentleman does not leave a lady in the desert alone."

"And what century are you from again?" Giselle taunted Taylor.

"Look. I don't like your crush at all, but you're crushing hard. If he's not treating you good, I'm going to make his life hell."

"First of all, no. I am not crushing on him."

Taylor held up a finger to shush Giselle. "Um, yeah, you are. You've been drooling all over that boy since you laid eyes on him."

"And I'm over it," Giselle said, with all the conviction of a jilted woman.

Taylor rolled her eyes. "No, you're not."

"Yes. I am."

"I saw the way you scanned the parking lot for his car when we got here. When we walked past his locker, you took a deep breath. You might be mad at him, but sweetie… you're crushing, hard!"

"Okay. Yeah. I looked for his car…because I want to throw a rock at it."

"See? Exaggerated anger. You just proved my point."

Damn her! Taylor was right. Despite her anger, a small bit of her was eager to lay eyes on Asher again. He was just so damn good-looking. Maybe not boyfriend material, but daydream worthy. And she did want to make him feel like a total ass by showing him her scars. He deserved that at the very least. "Fine. You're right. I'm going to go make him pay."

"Want me to come with you?"

"No. Guilt trips are what I'm good at." Giselle wandered off in the direction she'd last seen Asher go. He was heading for the cafeteria, probably in search of breakfast.

The cafeteria was surprisingly busy this early, filled with seniors who had first period free. She instantly spotted Asher in the line for breakfast and sauntered up, grabbing a tray and cutting him in the line.

He didn't say anything, but the sigh he let out was more growl than exhale. Good. She had his attention. She'd been forced to put a scarf around her neck to cover the wounds and knew as soon as she took it off, he'd see. Casually tugging at the end, she pulled it from her neck and set it on her tray, moving slowly with the line.

And right on cue, he noticed. "What the hell is that?" Anger and shock mingled together to raise the tone of his voice. "Who did that?"

"This?" Giselle thought for a second, wanting to choose her words carefully. "This… was a warning."

She could hear his nostrils flaring in anger. "Martina did this?"

She turned on him, glaring with all the inner Alpha she had within her. "No, you moron. Had you not been such a hot head and left me, you'd have seen him for yourself."

Asher's jaw dropped. "You found him?"

"He. Found. Me."

"Giselle… I…." Oh, god, could he look any hotter? Concern looked good on him. Giselle had to remind herself she was mad. Angry. Furious. He was the reason she was hurt. Well, part of it. She had to maintain the anger.

"Don't bother. I learned a valuable lesson."

"If I'd have thought…. I am so sorry." He was tripping

over himself to get the words out. "Please. Let me make it up to you. You need to have those wounds looked at… you need… herbs."

What she needed were wolves she could trust to be at her side, but apparently that was too much to ask. "I can't go to Martina. She can't know I went out after her warning. They'll just have to heal on their own."

"Please. Let me. I fight with my brothers all the time. I know the herbs. Let me at least do that much. You can hate me after that, okay?"

Against her better judgment, she agreed. He was so hard to resist. And doubly so when he was acting all protecting and caring. "Fine." She crossed her arms and stared down at him. "When?"

"Meet me for lunch. We'll go back to my house and I can make you a poultice."

"What the hell is a pol ice?"

He smiled at her mispronunciation. "Old-fashioned herbal bandaid."

"Hippy crap?"

"Yeah. Sure. Go with that."

So wolves were not only Neanderthal beasts, they were hippy tree-huggers too. Good to know. She had to fight the smile at her joke, not wanting Asher to think she was letting him off the hook or anything like that. She was still mad. Very mad at the ass for leaving her in the desert. "You know, I shouldn't keep ditching school. They're going to report me…"

"We'll be back in time. I promise. I have all the herbs there."

"You better have me back on time, then." Giselle turned and walked away, certain she'd made her point.

"Hey," Asher called after her.

She wasn't going to do it. She would not be at his beck

and call. Nope. Not turning around. She'd said she'd meet him at lunch and not a moment sooner.

Asher came running up behind her. "Stop."

"I'll see you at lunch."

"If anyone else sees those bites, you'll be seeing the health office and getting to visit CPS."

Damn. Trying to be cool, she'd forgotten her scarf. Giselle turned around and snatched the thin wispy cloth from his hands. "Thanks." And made a quick escape before her face turned completely red with embarrassment.

Taylor caught up with Giselle as she headed to class. She must have been waiting the entire time. Nice to see someone had her back. "Did you give him a good piece of your mind?"

"He says he can help with the bites," Giselle whispered.

"Really?"

"Yeah. Said he fights with his brothers all the time, knows about wolf bites."

"Well, I guess he's not all bad. But remember, while he's doctoring you up, if he hadn't left, you wouldn't have gotten hurt. Stay mad. Stay strong… sister."

Giselle couldn't hold back the giggle. "Yes, mother."

"If you'd just accept Martina, you'd have a mother."

"Oooh. Was that the tough sell?"

"Sorry, but we want you to be our sister. Di and I both. We like you."

"Where is Di today? She was gone before I woke up." Giselle hadn't given much thought to her other would-be sister until Tay mentioned her.

"Auditions for the spring production. She'll either be ecstatic or horribly depressed when the cast list goes up. Just a warning."

"Well, at least I won't have her breathing down my neck for a bit. Too preoccupied with being a star."

"I'll just have to do it for the both of us. Because we do want you to be our sister!"

"I just want to get to the bottom of this mess and clear the air. If we can prove Martina is not a threat, why can't the packs find peace? And then I can join you with a clear conscience."

"Whatever. Just remember who's filling your head with doubt, okay?" Taylor sighed.

"I'm not having this conversation any longer," Giselle grumbled and turned into her classroom, thankful to have fifty minutes of non-wolf topics to think about. Though when she read the board and saw there was a pop quiz, her mood soured.

21

Lunchtime had come faster than she'd expected, and Giselle's stomach fluttered like the wings of a thousand butterflies as she approached Asher's truck. Her head said she needed to stay mad at him, no matter what. But as she looked at the handsome wolf leaning against the truck and saw the outline of his pecs through his shirt, and remembered what he looked like naked... she had a hard time listening to her head. And his offer to help heal her wounds was a sign of good faith. How could he have truly known she was in danger... right?

Damn it! Giselle couldn't keep her thoughts straight.

She took a deep breath and squared her shoulders as she met up with him, hoping to give off a 'no funny business' vibe.

"Ready?" he asked, and she could count on one hand the times he'd given her a genuine smile. This one shocked her. So too did the note of hopefulness in his voice.

"Let's hurry. I don't want to miss any more school," Giselle said curtly, trying desperately to hold onto that justified anger.

"I didn't take you for someone with scholarly ambitions." He chuckled innocently enough, but it didn't smooth the sting of his insult.

Well, that comment really helped to fuel her anger. He must have really thought low of her to say some crap like that. "Actually, I have always been a straight A student, despite my upbringing and the unfortunate nature of my condition."

"Whoa, there. I didn't mean anything. I was just…"

"Making an ass out of yourself? You're pretty good at that, from what I've seen so far."

"Okay, I probably deserve that one. How many times will I have to apologize before you'll forgive me?"

"I'm not sure. There's no Miss Manners' guide for leaving someone to die in the desert with a potentially feral lone wolf lurking around."

He turned his eyes to the road and continued driving without another word. They pulled into a gated neighborhood with large lovely houses and huge front yards. Martina's house was not tiny, but in comparison, it seemed a shack now. The house they pulled up in front of had a three-car garage and what looked like a casita. Between the garage and casita was a gated entry to a large courtyard with pavers, a fire pit, and a rock wall fountain. Giselle was floored by the opulence. Rather than a typical front door (should she have expected anything less), the grand entrance came from a set of stark white French doors with stained glass accents. She was almost afraid to touch the doorknob and leave fingerprints, let alone walk inside and mark up the floor with her sneakers.

Asher waved her in without any apprehension and threw his bag down against the wall.

The outside of the house had wowed her, but the inside was just beyond words. Gorgeous marble floor. Accent walls painted in striking colors. Who knew red could look so good in a kitchen? Especially when that kitchen had a stone surround hiding the vent over the six-burner gas range. Damn. Even the granite countertops looked like something out of a magazine. And that was only one room. Dare she ask for a tour? *No. Stick to being mad. Stick to the plan. Poultice…whatever that was… and get back to school.*

"Through here," Asher called over his shoulder without looking behind to see if she was following. "Help yourself to anything in the fridge if you want."

Sure, she could use a soda… if she could find the fridge. All she saw were honey-colored wood cabinets with silver knobs. Did they conjure up some kind of magic to make their refrigerator appear and disappear?

Asher had walked into a sort of arched hallway between the kitchen and the dining room. At least she hoped it was the dining room. She couldn't be sure, as there was either a table or another counter matching the same granite as the kitchen in there.

Asher glanced over and must have caught her confused expression. "Last cabinet to the right. Grab me a soda too, will ya?" He continued to rummage around in drawers in the hallway and Giselle turned to randomly opening up cabinets to find this mysterious fridge.

Sure enough, hidden to look like the rest of the cabinets and pantry, was a full-size refrigerator stocked with drinks. She grabbed two sodas and followed Asher to the short hallway.

"Turn around and pull off your scarf." His tone was just as curt as hers had been in the truck. Maybe he was giving her a taste of her own medicine, or maybe this was just how he acted. Their first meeting sounded something like that, personality-free and rude.

She did as he asked, and before she was ready, he slapped something down on her wounds that was both icy and searing at the same time. She hissed more from the shock than anything else, but as the searing heat began to seep into her skin, she had to pant to keep the scream of pain at bay.

"Yeah, doesn't feel very good," he said just as curtly as before. "But it will help. I'm putting three of them across your neck and securing them with a bit of tape. You'll need the scarf for cover for the rest of the day, but everything should be fine after your next shift."

If the pain kept up, she might not make it through the rest of the day. She tried to use her voice to say something, anything, but all she could let out without wailing was a sharp squeak.

"The pain will go away. I promise."

Sure... like she was going to believe him. He could have at least warned her about how it would feel.

"Breathe, Giselle. Or you'll pass out."

Damn. The way her name rolled off his tongue, she almost forgot her anger. If she had a voice, she might have asked him to repeat himself.

"You have to relax. Breathe through the pain. It will go away in a few moments."

She couldn't breathe. She couldn't speak. The pain was overwhelming.

Asher spun her around and before she knew what was happening, planted a kiss on her lips that melted away everything that was bothering her. He held her tight against him, and lightheaded as she had just become, she was thankful for his support. But strong arms were the last thing on her mind at the moment. Those luscious lips and the heady masculine scent filling her nose were taking over all her senses.

Almost as quickly as his lips had found hers, he pulled back and met her eyes. "Still hurting?"

Surprisingly, she wasn't. "No." Her voice had returned too.

"Told you. Just needed to give the herbs time to settle in. You'll be fine for the rest of the day."

And just like that, he closed up a box, put it back in the drawer, and headed through the kitchen. "Let's go. Don't want to be late for class."

Dumbfounded. There was nothing else to describe how she felt at that moment. Like a switch, he went from hot to cold as if nothing had happened, while she simmered with the remainder of unspent passion for a man… a boy she shouldn't even want.

The entire silent ride back to school was spent with her dwelling on just that thought, while Asher seemed unaffected.

What was his deal? First he acted like she was lower than dirt. Then he tried to be her friend, maybe more, and then suddenly, after getting his nose whacked, metaphorically speaking, he switched gears yet again. Maybe the girls were right. He was no good. Too bad, though; he had potential to be great.

"Thanks," she said hopping down from the truck when they parked back at school.

"Be careful."

She was almost shocked to hear his voice, he'd been silent so long.

"I will." Giselle shouldered her bag, forgetting her wounds, but was instantly reminded by the pain. She whimpered quietly, trying to hide how bad it really hurt, but Asher's keen hearing had to have picked it up.

And he was at her back in a second. "Stand still." He checked her dressings, and then took the bag from her hands. "I'll carry this."

"Really, you don't have to."

"Yes, I do. You're going to rip your wounds open if I don't."

She was about to argue some more, but decided just to let him. It was nice to have someone help, even if he was mixing his signals so much he was making her head spin.

"You confuse me, you know that, right?"

"No more than you do me," he snickered.

"What do you have to be confused about?" Her thoughts turned quickly back to the kiss. It had felt so nice, and yet he'd switched off all emotion the second it was over.

"Nothing." Stoicism was back in his expression and tone. Another confusing signal.

"Great. Now that that's settled. Oh, look, there's Diana!" She snatched her bag from Asher's grip, slung it over her undamaged side, and left him without another word.

Di, on the other hand, looked as if she had more than a few for Giselle.

"Do you want to be part of this pack or not?" Her tone spoke volumes about her anger, even if only Giselle could hear it. Thankfully the rest of the kids in the hall were too occupied with their own lives to eavesdrop on her lecture.

"You know I do. I am just doing my... homework."

"Where were you at lunch?"

She hadn't told Di about her back. And unconsciously, her hand went to her neck, fingers caressing the scarf concealing her wounds. "I needed to step out for some real food. You know the cafeteria doesn't cut it during that time of the month. I needed real meat."

Di snorted, clearly not convinced. "I could have gone too."

"Sorry. I'm not used to thinking like a pack."

"And you never will if you keep this up." Di sounded more hurt than angry, but Giselle was in no mood to rehash

the same conversation they'd been havi...
many times would they need to go round
topic? If this was what being in a pack wa...

She was never more thankful to see Ms. Freeman call
the class to order.

"Gotta go." Giselle squeezed past Di and headed into
the room.

She practically threw herself into her seat without even a
passing glance at Damien. He'd not missed her rough
entrance at all, however. "Fighting with your sister already?"

"Don't ask," Giselle huffed.

"But I did ask. And the offer still stands if you want to
ride with me this weekend."

Ash walked into class and took his seat, glancing back
quickly at Giselle.

She turned away from him, still utterly confused by
what had happened over lunch. "What? Where?" She'd
completely forgotten she'd made any plans.

"I'm hurt." Damien sounded anything but hurt, but the
words brought her attention right where he wanted… on
him. "Mount Charleston? Skiing? Ring any bells?"

"Shit. Yes. Sorry. Bad day. Don't think I'm a bitch or
anything."

"Language, Ms. Richards," Ms. Freeman barked at her
from the front of the class. "And let's all please come to
order."

Giselle glanced quickly over to Damien and those irresistible puppy-dog eyes. "I'm still riding with Diana and
Taylor, but I'm looking forward to seeing you."

Not the answer he'd been hoping for; that was evident
by the hard line of his jaw. But he'd have to accept it. She
was not ready to play games with more than one boy, and
Ash was already screwing with her mind.

22

Finally, after what had felt like an endless week, the weekend arrived.

It never snowed in Vegas, or so they said, but only an hour away there was a winter wonderland awaiting. Frosty little flakes of white floated down to an already blanketed mountainside as the car snaked through twists and turns on the scenic route up towards the ski resort. Giselle watched with nervous anticipation as they neared their destination. Her mind was still occupied with questions, and the girls had passed the point of annoyance with her. The last couple of days had dragged on. But this was meant to be a fun outing and a chance to leave behind the problems of the city and have a little carefree time in the snow. Still, the entire ride up, the conversation had been poignantly guided toward things other than wolves. Taylor had made it a point to toss some of her magazines at Giselle and have her circle outfit ideas she thought would be cute as a task to keep her quiet.

When they finally arrived in the parking lot, Giselle practically flung herself to the ground she got out so quickly. The parking lot was well salted and slushy but very the snow still falling, she worried she'd be frozen to the bone in no time.

pulled her snowboard from the roof and shouldered her bag. "See you all later."

"What, no escort today?" Giselle had attempted to be funny, but as usual came out as a bitch.

"You're perfectly capable of handling yourself," Tay said, walking away without looking back.

"Did I pick the wrong outfit or something?" Giselle asked Di.

"Really, Captain Obvious? Quit being a smart ass. We all need a break from each other today, so let's just do that." Di turned and headed for the lodge.

She should have expected as much from Di, but to have Taylor giving her the cold shoulder was a bit disconcerting. There was more chill in the air than the snow was providing, that was for sure. Giselle shrugged to herself and zipped her coat up, covering her mouth.

The lodge looked inviting enough – small compared to what she'd expected, but warm, and that was what counted. She headed that way when a familiar voice called out to her. "Giselle!"

She didn't recognize him at first. Behind the beanie, sun glasses, and heavy coat, he could have been anybody, but the voice was distinctly Damian's. A friendly face she was happy to see after the cold shoulders of this morning.

"Ready to go tubing?"

"I was thinking of warming up."

"I know you're not the girly girl type like Di. You can handle a little fun in the snow."

"How is it you know so much about Di? Did you two…?"

"Oh, no. Nothing like that. We're…."

"Friends?"

"Acquaintances, really."

"And yet, you know so much about her."

"I did her a favor a while back. She's been cool ever since."

"You mean a witchy favor."

"Shhhhh." He touched a finger to her lips, and it sent a chill that had nothing to do with the cold racing down her spine. "Doctor-patient confidentiality."

"The what now?" She pushed his finger away.

"Yes. Witchy business, as you so cutely put it."

"Not allowed to talk about it, or something?"

"Magical contract. No one is able to divulge secrets of what happens when money exchanges hands for witchy work."

"Or you'll turn into a toad?"

"Funny. Really funny. If only that were the case. No, witches who snitch are no longer witches."

"That's a cute little rhyme. You make that one up yourself?"

"Keep talking, Snarky, and I'll turn you into a frog."

"Can you do that?" She was actually curious, but her tone failed to convey the truth.

"Hold up, let me grab my wand and show you."

"Seriously?"

"Wow. Gullible much?"

"Jerk." She smacked his arm.

"I'm guessing you don't know much about any others, do you?"

"Uh… Hello? Foster kid. I don't even know about myself, let alone others. I've been getting lectured over and over for my loner habits."

"Yeah, your kind are supposed to be pack animals."

"Really? Thanks, Captain Obvious."

"Always here to help." He puffed his chest and Giselle

smacked him on it.

"Whatever."

"Aww, don't be like that. I'm just playing with you." He grabbed hold of her and squeezed tightly.

She hadn't expected the hug, or expected she'd like being held so tight by someone, but his arms around her felt... nice. She relaxed into his hold and tried to let herself just be in the moment.

"Playing is okay. But no magical funny business... you hear me?"

He snorted as he let her go. "Well, I better pack it in now, because aside from my terrible game, funny business is all I got."

"I'd say you were doing pretty good so far... with the normal funny business. But no croaking."

Even through the sunglasses, she caught the smile rising all the way to his eyes. "How about we amp things up then? C'mon." He grabbed hold of her hand and tugged her away from the lodge.

"No. Wait. Warmth," she whimpered as he dragged her along.

"I'll keep you warm."

Wasn't that a promising thought? He wasn't Asher, and she cursed herself for even thinking of that boy while in Damien's company, but he did have his own magnetism. And better still, he was not conflicted at all about what he wanted. That in itself was worth a whole heck of a lot of bonus points. Not to mention how snuggly she'd just felt in his arms. So random, but oh, so nice!

He brought her down to where others were sliding down a small but steep enough hill. "C'mon, I have a tube all set up for us."

She really didn't have a choice; he practically threw her down on a large back inner tube and hopped on with her.

Down the hill they went before she could catch her breath. They came to a slushy halt down at the bottom.

"See? Fun." He beamed and hoisted the tube, ready to take it back up the hill again.

She had to admit it was fun, though it would have been nice for him to let her catch her breath first before sending them hurtling down the mountain. But she'd forgive him this once.

Giselle chased after him, up the hill, and they set up for round two.

A solid hour they spent sliding and hiking and sliding again, each time bringing more laughs and louder squeals from Giselle than the one prior.

"I knew you'd have fun."

"I have to admit, I had not counted on it being this much fun."

"Ouch… I'm hurt." He pantomimed being hit in the chest with an arrow straight into his heart and collapsed on the ground.

"Get up, you big baby. I didn't mean it like that. I've just never been great with the social scene. I usually embarrass myself."

"You mean like you did just there, insulting me and my day of fun and snowball fighting?"

"What?" She'd hardly had time to get the word out before he pinged her with a ball of slush in her stomach.

"Heads up." He tossed another one, hitting her in the shoulder.

"Oh, you're going to pay for that one." She picked up a handful and after packing it down into a quick ball, beaned him right in the forehead with it.

"Dead eye! Good to know." He rolled out of the way and found a tree to hide behind.

"You think that will save you?"

"Nope, just give me a minute to reload." He fired off two quick snowballs at her, but this time Giselle was able to duck out of the way.

She bobbed and weaved as he tossed more her way and returned her own volley of fast repetition slush balls. Damn that tree for getting in the way! "Come out and face me like a man, you coward."

"Insulting my manhood… that's a low blow, even for you." He stepped out from behind the tree and faced her. Without moving his arms he managed to launch three snowballs at her. When she returned fire, her snowballs exploded as if impacting something – yet they hadn't touched him.

"Not fair… I said no witchy funny business." She crouched low, narrowing her eyes, focusing to see if there was an edge to his magical barrier, wondering to herself how strong the barrier was and if she might be able to penetrate it.

"You're too good. I had to even the odds."

"Liar. You just wanted to show off." She could find no visible trace of his barrier, no sign of where it might begin or end.

"I did. Do you blame a guy for trying to show off in front of a cute girl?" He casually stepped forward, one foot in front of the other, but whether or not it was caution or arrogance that slowed his pace, she couldn't tell.

And she didn't like not knowing.

His eyes had changed too. Gone was the beauty and the innocence she'd been captivated by. They were sharper, darker, more focused. He was concentrating hard to keep that barrier going. She could sense the effort it took. Awe inspiring in a way to see a live witch in action, but frightening all the same.

Still, though, her wolf was on alert, the hair on the back

of her neck rising in apprehension, the possible threat causing her wolf to rise up even without her allowing it. She crouched lower involuntarily as her wolf came forward to protect her.

Damien must have caught the change. In a matter of seconds, the darkness in his eyes faded. "Sorry, Giselle. I didn't... please, calm down. I was only playing."

Barely aware of how far into the change she was, Giselle regained control and sent her wolf back, standing a little wobbly upright again. "You can't challenge a wolf like that without being ready to meet it."

"Honestly, I am so sorry. I didn't expect..." His words trailed off as he held his hand out in surrender.

"Haven't you dealt with Di or any other wolf before?"

"Just the human side. Damn. You're scary as a wolf, has anyone ever told you that?"

"Yeah. It's kind of the point."

"Right... Sorry. I really am." He looked like he wanted to reach out and take her hand or maybe give her a hug or something involving physical contact, but the wolf, still too close to the surface, had her pulling back as if his touch would burn her. "What were you trying to do, anyway?"

"I was going to bury you in snowballs... as a joke."

"Funny."

"It was supposed to be."

She glared at him.

"How about a cup of hot chocolate instead?"

It was a paltry peace offering, but she had to accept it. Though her wolf was still clawing away anxiously inside of her, she knew, or at least hoped, that Damien had been just playing a bad joke. He was a boy, after all. And Di had no problem with him, so he couldn't be all that bad. People made mistakes. Hell, she was well known for making them herself, and if she could get her wolf to calm, the hot chocolate might smooth out the rest. "Okay. No more funny business, witch."

"Damn. Now you're saying it like it's a bad thing."

"From where I'm standing, it is."

"I promise. I meant no harm. And anything stronger than a snowball would have hit me too, so you should have just pegged me in the head with a rock and dragged my lifeless body off into the woods as punishment. Seriously. I deserved it."

"Calm down, melodramatic man."

"Who just screwed up a perfect afternoon with the hottest new girl in school."

She blushed at the compliment. Even when he was playing the martyr, he was still smooth. "I'm cold. Let's get that hot chocolate."

They walked back up to the lodge, and Giselle grabbed a table by the wall of windows. The snow had stopped and the sun was shining, making everything glisten with a fresh new powder coat. Skiers and snowboarders came in and out at random, picking up mugs of hot stuff and slugging it down as if it were their last drink on earth. Giselle caught sight of Di entertaining a group in the corner; she nodded but didn't wave. Di had made it clear they needed an afternoon off, and she was happy about it now. Somehow seeing her in the corner had suddenly added a weight to the room that hadn't been there before.

Damien returned with steaming mugs in hand. "You look like a marshmallow kind of girl."

"Good guess." She took a ginger sip of from the hot mug, enjoying the sting of it against her frozen lips. Instantly she felt warmer, but not warm enough yet to strip off her coat. That would take a few more sips at least.

"So, am I forgiven?"

"Maybe." Damn, just seeing Di sitting there in the corner brought all her worries back.

Damien looked over his shoulder and caught sight of Di too. He waved and she nodded back at him.

"You guys having sister issues?"

"We're not sisters."

"Yet, right? I mean, you're living with them. You have to join the pack."

Giselle shrugged.

"What's up? Earlier this week, when you arrived, you all seemed inseparable, and now…"

"Can I be honest with you?" She hadn't meant to blurt it out, but it was there niggling at the back of her mind.

He pulled back, caught off guard by her sudden tone. "I guess. What's up?"

"What do you really know about the two wolf packs issues? I know they had a witch do something."

"Doctor-patient confidentiality… remember? I couldn't find out even if I wanted to."

"Someone has to know. I found this statue in the desert, hidden in cave. Only it isn't a statue. I think it was a wolf, and someone…"

"Used some magical funny business…"

"Yep."

"I can't confirm anything, because I don't know… honestly. But it's possible. There are spells that can turn a living being to stone. Nasty stuff, though, and not cheap if someone was trying to buy a witch off to do it."

"But are there witches here that would do it?"

"Any witch *can*. The magic is there."

"But that's like bad witch stuff, right?"

"Bad, good, it's really just a label. Magic is magic."

"But turning someone to stone is just evil."

"Yeah, I agree. Not nice at all. But the magic to do it is neither bad nor good."

That was a distinction she couldn't wrap her head around. When would turning someone to stone not be a bad thing? Was there anyone alive that deserved it?

"Are they still alive, or dead when this happens?" Giselle was almost scared to learn the answer.

"My guess, and it's only a guess, I'm still learning, is that they are frozen. Neither alive nor dead. If it could be reversed, they'd not have any memory of the time they were a statue."

"So, it could be reversed?"

"In theory. You thinking of hiring someone to try?"

"Like I could afford it…"

Damien shrugged. "Probably not."

"I just feel like there is this weight hanging over my decision to join or not join the Hernandez family. They're nice enough…"

"Well, then what's stopping you?"

"Ash." She hadn't meant it to come out the way it did, and instantly she saw Damien's guard go up. "He said something… about the two packs… and war."

Too late. Just the mention of his name had Damien turned off. Gone was the carefree smile and the confidence. "Yeah. They're at war, and probably will be forever."

"If I tie myself to a pack in a war… It's just not appealing."

"Sometimes in life you just have to choose a side and run with it."

There was way more subtext in his words than she was ready to deal with. Damn testosterone ran thick with boys. Even non-wolfboy seemed to have that territorial vibe with ferocity.

"See, that's the thing. I'm a lone wolf. Always have been. I live by my wits and instincts. Not by the will of others." She hoped her words with their equal measure of subtext got through to him.

"You do what you have to do, I guess." He shrugged. Whether he got the message or not, she couldn't tell. He sipped his hot chocolate and stared out of the window, as if hoping to find something more interesting out there.

"That's the thing. My instincts tell me to make peace and then decide. If only I could." She sighed.

A few moments went by in silence, both of them working on their drinks and looking anywhere but each other. She'd all but given up hope on the day when Damien finished his cocoa and set his mug down a bit harder than normal.

"I might be able to help."

She cocked her head to the side, a wolfy reflex. "Really? How?"

"I can't find out who did what, but I might be able to look into counter-spells."

"You'd do that?"

"No promises. But I can look into it. Maybe your statue theory is real, and the wolf behind it will have some answers for you."

Giselle's eyes lit up, and she reached across the table and grabbed hold of Damien's hands, squeezing tightly. "Thank you."

"Don't thank me yet. And don't expect miracles. I make no promises about anything."

"Right. Of course."

"But you have to promise me something, too…"

"What's that?"

"This has to be our secret. No one can know what's going on. Not your family. And especially not Ash."

She hesitated for a moment before accepting his terms, wondering why he singled out Ash specifically. It had to do deeper than territorial male bs. "Yeah. Okay. Our secret."

"I'm serious."

"I won't tell anyone."

"Not until the deed is done, or I have an answer on whether or not it can be."

They shook on it, and Giselle could feel his hand almost vibrating with energy. She sensed that though nothing was on paper, they'd just entered into some kind of magical contract. That unnerved her a bit, as she was still unclear the capabilities of her witchy friend or his nature: good or bad. He might have said there was really no distinction, but people who could do despicable things were bad, no questions asked, and she'd rather not align herself that way.

Di walked up just as their hands parted. "Is this a business meeting or what? You too look so glum."

Giselle smiled up at her sister. "Just recounting my sob story… you know, life on the run. No home. Blah, blah, blah."

"And I told her she has me all day and night…" Damien the playboy was back.

"Be careful with him, Elle, he's a fast one." She winked and walked away.

"See, she approves." Damien's smile returned, thankfully.

Giselle stopped herself from saying what she wanted to: that Di was just happy to keep her from Ash. It might be a bit awkward in the current company. "She's happy to see me talking to other people."

"Enough talking. Let's go play some more. The snow's calling."

23

Things settled down over the next few days. Giselle's wounds healed, and Martina had all but forgotten her little runaway attempt, or at least pretended to. Even the girls had let up on their crusade to push her into a decision. The weekend excursion to the mountain had done everyone good. A sense of normalcy had descended upon most of the house – but not Giselle. Though she felt some peace of mind knowing that Damien would help her possibly find out more about the wolf statue, she was still no closer to the answers surrounding the two families or the strange wolf in the desert, and she couldn't help but wonder at a possible connection.

Risking another trip into the desert wouldn't be smart, especially after the lone wolf's warning. And she wasn't keen to reopen those wounds that had just healed. Knowing the girls were happy not to ever bring up the subject again, she was at a loss as to what to do.

How long could she put it off before they forced her to make a decision? She couldn't hope for them to keep her until she came of age, could she? Too many questions. What should have been a time of peace was filled with these nagging questions, and as she stared blankly at the bed above hers, she knew another night of insomnia awaited. Might as well get some more studying in while she had the time.

Giselle crept down into the living room with her algebra book and notepad, expecting to find it empty, but as she hit the last step, Gavin's voice nearly made her jump.

"Taking off again?" Curiosity rather than annoyance colored his tone.

"Yeah, secret math club meeting." She held up her book.

He smiled, and even in the dark, she could see relief washing over his face. He must have really thought her a runner. That spoke volumes about how they really saw her. "All the cool kids are in Trig, eh?" Despite what he might be thinking, his tone remained cool and calm.

"One day... one day...," she giggled.

She hadn't really spent much one-on-one time with Gavin. A foreman for a local homebuilder, he was a workaholic, gone most of the day and often late into the evening. But their limited interactions had been nice enough. And the girls loved him like a father.

"Can't sleep?" he asked.

"Never... anymore." She must have been tired to blurt that out the way she had.

"I've got the cure for that." He held up a mug. "You want some tea? Chamomile... Martina swears by the stuff."

"Sure." She'd give anything for a night of good rest. Setting her book and notepad on the bar, she scooted up onto a stool and watched Gavin put the mug of water in the microwave.

"I'd ask if you wanted to talk, but I know you're not going to."

Well, that was an odd way to start a conversation, but

Giselle had never been happier to hear those words. Everyone else in the house had been hell bent on getting to the bottom of her issues. The no-pressure approach was refreshing and actually made her trust him that much more.

Gavin pulled out a box of tea and a mesh infuser. "I was a lone wolf once... Did Martina ever tell you?"

She had, and Giselle appreciated it. Just one more way in which she fit in with this group. They were all, to some extent, lone wolves. As far as his place in the pack was concerned, Gavin was the strong but very silent Alpha partner. Martina did most of the mothering and organizing of pack business, whereas Gavin seemed to be content to go along with her lead.

The microwave beeped. He pulled out the steaming cup of water, placed the infuser inside, and set the timer for three minutes. "Yep. Thought I'd be a loner for life until I met Martina. She's quite special."

"You two make a wonderful couple." She wasn't sure where he was going, but felt she had to say something to avoid looking rude.

"Thanks. But I wasn't fishing. Just pointing something out. I know what you're going through. Pack life isn't for all wolves, despite what everyone else will tell you. Some wolves just don't belong in a pack."

Was she one of them, and was he saying this to her as a gentle nudge to get out?

"Perhaps I'm one of those wolves." She shrugged. Not the worst thing to admit to.

"Only you can know that. But..." He set a honey bear in front of her and the steaming cup of tea on the counter. "Whatever decisions you make for or against being part of a pack have to come from here." He pointed to his heart. "You can't be forced. And your wolf certainly won't stand for it. It all has to feel right."

"Thanks." She spoke cautiously, not sure what the right thing to say was.

Gavin leaned his large frame against the tile counter and watched Giselle for a moment. She could see the wolf underneath his gaze, curious more than calculating, but watchful all the same. "Now, don't let that stuff scare you. I'm not talking about you being in my pack right now."

He'd hit the nail right on the head, and she was relieved he was not giving her the old heave ho.

"I'm talking about how you feel about being part of any pack. If your heart isn't in it, you cannot commit. Nor should you." His words were exactly what she needed to hear. The girls had been on her since day one. Martina had been almost sickeningly sweet in her own attempts to sway Giselle. It had all been too much given the questions she'd had, causing everyone own grief. Gavin's words were a breath of fresh air.

"But what about you all?"

"If that's what is stressing you out so much you can't sleep, then stop. You do not have to be part of my pack to stay under my roof."

Those words released all kinds of pent up tension that had been building within her. But despite that relief, she had to wonder if there was some underlying motive. Now things were fitting together a little too perfectly. "Why are you so understanding?"

"When I was a kid, I was abandoned. I grew up on the streets and had to make my own way. I'd have given my left eye for a family, but none ever came. When I was older and had made something of myself, I knew I did not need that family to support me. I met quite a few good packs along the way, and none were for me."

"And then you met Martina?"

He smiled. "Drink your tea."

She poured some honey into her cup and pulled out ட infuser, setting it on a plate. "Love at first sight?"

Gavin chuckled. "Quite the opposite. She was insufferable. A gigantic pain in my ass."

Giselle took a sip of her tea, enjoying the way it warmed her as it traveled down her throat. "So how did she change you into a pack man?"

"She needed me. She was in a very bad place and coming unraveled. The two packs were at a full-scale war. She'd just lost her sister and her father. Then the pack war claimed her mother and one of her brothers too in less than a month's time. The rest of the family, cousins and aunts and uncles, were driven off, and poor Martina was left to be a loner herself. She refused to leave, and if I hadn't helped, she might have been a goner too."

"So you didn't join a pack…"

"I created one."

"What about Martina's family? The rest of the pack?"

"Scattered, dead, who knows? The war with the Thrace clan really did a number on her family."

"But why?"

"Old man Thrace was the mob boss of Alphas."

"Asher's father?" she mumbled, not intending for Gavin to hear.

"No. His grandfather. There was supposed to be a joining of the packs, but Martina's sister didn't want to marry. Old man Thrace got wind of it, and when the wedding didn't happen, feelings got hurt and he called in some nasty favors…"

"Magical favors?" Giselle's thoughts turned to the wolf statue in the cave.

"Sure, and plenty of violence. If you ask me, neither pack was playing fair, but that's not for me to say. When all was said and done, Martina was the only one left. Said she wouldn't go. Her sister had vanished and maybe she'd come back one day."

Giselle's eyes lit with excitement as she put the puzzle pieces together in her mind. "So she's not dead?"

Gavin let out a defeated breath. "I think she is. But Martina lives with hope. Her sister just vanished without a trace. It was in the early days of the war, but, if you ask me, I believe she was the first casualty."

"What was her name?"

"Christina."

"Pretty."

"She was Martina's twin."

"Does she have a grave marker or memorial? Someplace Martina can go to grieve her?"

"No. Martina says she believes her to still be alive. She's got that whole twin psychic link thing. That's why she won't leave town despite all the fighting. She hopes that one day she'll see her sister again."

Giselle took another sip of her tea. "I hope she does."

"I'm more practical about these things, but if it keeps her from breaking down, why not hold on to the dream?" Gavin leaned across the bar and whispered, "Don't tell her I said that, though. Our secret, okay?"

Giselle nodded, sipping her tea, trying to act as casual as she could when inside she was a bundle of energy. If what she hoped was true, that statue she'd found could be the key to it all. She had to find a way to see it again, and if Damien could find the spell... She might just burst with all the possibilities. "I'm all for keeping the peace. I guess that's part of my problem with joining a pack. I'm too much a free spirit. I need to run and be free. Feel the wind in my fur. You known what I mean?"

His expression changed, and the father in him showed quite clearly in his stern gaze. "Not safe for a pup. But you've already had that lecture."

"Martina told you?" She slumped in her seat, trying to look appropriately guilty enough to avoid round three of 'running in the desert' lectures.

"Of course she did. We are partners in all things. Including being your parent, guardian, or whatever you want to call us."

"You were a lone wolf once, so you understand."

"I do. But I cannot condone your running in the open desert with tension between the packs still running high."

"What if I stayed within our borders? What are our borders?"

"I still think it's a bad idea, but you and the girls together within our borders might be doable."

"That's not exactly a free run in the desert."

"No, but lone wolf or not, you'll have to make compromises until you're of age."

"I see. And if we were all to run... all us girls... what would be the boundaries?"

"Easier to show you, rather than say, but if you hit creek or mountains, you've gone too far, and obviously running in the city as a wolf is a big no-no. But luckily, the girls know the boundaries, so if you're running with them, you should be okay... in broad daylight."

Giselle giggled. "Got it... Only run though the neighborhood streets in broad daylight"

He narrowed his eyes in a very fatherly "I don't think so" stare.

"Joking!"

"I'm not giving my permission, just so we're clear; but if you and the girls have to run without us, stay away from the creek. That's out of bounds. "

"Understood."

"It's hard being a loner in a pack world. I more than

anyone else here understands, but try to work within the rules while you feel your new position out. No one will pressure you for an answer, okay?"

"I really appreciate that." It lifted the biggest weight of her shoulders having him confirm it.

Gavin nodded and headed out of the kitchen. "Finish your tea and head up to bed. Algebra can wait."

She took another big sip and let the warmth wash down her throat again. Whether it was Gavin's words or the tea's effect, she did feel calmer. Maybe now sleep would come.

A lone wolf howled in the distance.

Maybe not.

She wanted so much to go out and investigate, but knew better. Alone was never a good choice. Of course, no one said she had to be alone.

She ran upstairs and pulled her phone off the charger and texted Asher.

Elle: Want to redeem yourself?

She waited in anticipation, hoping he would answer, but after looking at the clock realized that might not happen. Past midnight, most people – or at least not insomniacs with insecurity issues – were in bed.

She shrugged, set the phone back down, and collapsed on her bed. Staring up at the bunk above her, she couldn't help but let her mind wander. The statue, the lone wolf, the two families. They were all so closely tied together, but what was the real story?

Just as she was finally in the arms of sleep's warm embrace, her cell chirped. She sprang from the bed and snatched it in one swipe.

Ash: I don't need redeeming.

Asshat! Of course he would say something so, so, jerky!

Elle: Nevermind!

She wanted to slam down the phone but thought better of it. Waking the other girls would just lead to drama. Downside to the whole pack thing – everything is everyone's business. Even insomnia!

The phone chirped again.
Ash: Are you drunk?

What the hell kind of question was that? She angrily punched in her answer.

Elle: No. Just wanted to talk, but you're too busy being a dick about everything.

Ash: You need to chill, seriously. I'm just messing with you. You did text me at midnight.

Elle: I want the truth. Your family's side of the story. The whole story this time.

Ash: This again?

Elle: Yep. Until I get to the bottom of it all.

Ash: You know everything I know.

Elle: Well, then I'm going to have to ask the lone wolf.

Ash: Don't go back there…

Elle: I have to. We're missing something big here. And I bet he knows. About that statue too.

Ash: Don't go alone.

Elle: Come with me… and stay with me this time.

For what felt like an eternity, the messages stopped. She knew his answer without him having to type it. He wouldn't come. And that was fine. That was exactly the reason he was no good… not for her, and not as a wolf either. She'd convince the girls to go with her in the next few days. As a group, they'd be in better shape to approach the loner anyway. Yeah. That was a better idea. She needn't bother with stupid Asher.

Ash: Fine. Tomorrow. Before school.

His response shocked her. School started at nine. If they got an early start at six, when the sun came up, they'd have plenty of time to make it back.

Elle: 6am. Same place. By the road.

Now she only needed to sneak out before the girls got wind.

24

Sleep never came. But that made it all the easier when sun began to peek over the mountains for Giselle to creep down the stairs and out the front door. A bit earlier than she'd intended to leave, but she wanted to ensure she didn't run into anyone in the house. No one was due up for at least two more hours. If she was lucky. She might even be back before Martina woke up to make breakfast.

Still chilly, Giselle couldn't wait to shift so her fur could keep her warm. The thin hoodie wasn't doing a very good job. She slipped out the back gate into the alleyway towards the open desert. There she could shift and run as far and fast as she would like.

She might have been early, but Asher's truck sitting along the road made her feel like she'd shown up fashionably late. She walked alongside it, feeling the cool metal body. He'd been there for longer than a few minutes; the truck was as cold as ice.

A quick look around didn't reveal any signs of Asher around, either. How long had he been out there? And then her stomach sank like a stone. *He hadn't tried to see the lone wolf himself, had he?*

That wolf had nearly ripped her to shreds, and she guessed the only reason he hadn't had nothing to do with the fact that she was a pup, but more likely that she was female. You'd have to be a pretty big jerk to kill a young girl wolf. Not that she saw herself as young or vulnerable, but the world had its own opinions, which had been forced on her every day of her foster kid life. Why fight them now? It was far better to let people think their own wrong ideas of you than to force them to see the truth anyway.

But Asher was a damn fool if he'd gone out without her.

She caught his scent before he came into view. There in the brush, eyes twinkling, was the tall, dark-haired wolf Asher staring back at her. Both relieved and ready to give him a good smack for being a jerk, she stripped down, shifted, and ran after him. Knowing she'd need her clothes later, she carried them in her mouth and headed off in a sprint.

She took the lead, heading straight toward the mountain to find the creek.

They ran swiftly through the desert, as the early morning sun lit up their path, and the creek came into view. Giselle turned to make sure Asher was still following. They were close to where she'd found the old loner, and just the thought of seeing him made her neck itch, right where he'd bitten her.

Asher was there, thankfully. That gave her some relief; but still, remembering the teeth and the size of that wolf gave her a chill. He'd said to never come back, and the smart thing would have been to listen. But they were here now, no point in letting fear take over. Giselle took off again, down along the water and toward the cave.

The small entrance appeared ahead, and still Giselle had not seen or smelled the other wolf. He was good. She hadn't smelled him before either, but he'd been there, the whole time, watching.

At the mouth of the cave, she dropped her clothes and shifted on the spot. "So, the wolf statue inside the cave," she asked, "Do you know anything about it?"

Asher shifted too, but he hadn't brought any clothes. Why, oh why, did he have to be so hot?

He shrugged and the ripples of his muscles made her weak in the knees. Damn! What was she asking him about? It took all the willpower she had to keep her eyes above the waist and remember why they were out there.

"Probably some casino discard, and stupid kids brought it out to the desert for…who knows what."

A likely story… not. He knew more than he was letting on, she was certain of it. But Asher was as closed off as they come, and for no good reason, either. Why come out all this way if not to help clear the air?

"Try again, wolfboy. You saw the wolf statue. It's in perfect condition. Or better yet, go inside and have another look for yourself. "

He didn't make a move for the cave. Just stood there, defiantly still. Yep, he knew more than he was letting on, and she'd have to put all her cunning to good use to make him talk.

"Maybe they haven't had time to vandalize it yet?"

She gave him her best "What am I, stupid?" look.

"What do you want me to say? I don't know what it is or why it's here."

Liar, liar, pants on fire! She could sense it, but he excelled at stonewalling the direct approach. So, Giselle would have to go the long way. "Fine. What's the story with old man Thrace?"

The innocent way his head tilted sideways almost made her trust the way he mumbled the word, "Dad?"

"No. I want to know about Grandpa."

Asher's tightening jaw was the dead giveaway she needed.

"Busted… spill! I want details. What's your Grandpa's issue?"

Despite being caught knowing more than he was letting on, Asher still maintained his stoic look of defiance. "He's a hot head… or was."

"Dead?"

"Yep."

"How'd he go?"

"Surprisingly, old age. Though it wasn't for lack of trying."

"Many enemies?"

"Yep. He had quite the turnout at his funeral last year."

Her eyebrow quirked. "Recently deceased. Okay. So what was his role in the family feud?"

Asher shrugged, and she followed that casual ripple of movement down his chest and… *Damn it, Giselle, stay focused!*

Asher wasn't playing fair, and he knew it. He cracked the slightest of smiles catching her eyes drift south. But just as soon as it appeared, the amusement left his face again. "Grandfather set up the arranged marriage, from what I was told. It failed; feelings got hurt."

"But your dad got blamed for the fallout."

"Dad's no pushover, but what he was accused of is child's play compared to what Grandpa was capable of."

"So, what did grandpa do? Don't lie, I can smell it on you. You reek of anxiety right now."

He didn't like being called out. If Giselle wasn't mistaken, there was a slight growl rumbling though his very handsome chest. And those eyes of his had turned to ice. He locked onto her with an Alpha's domineering gaze, but she wasn't playing that game.

"There's no use in games, Ash. Just be truthful."

"Yes. Dad got accused of using a witch to help get revenge, but... I think – and I am not sure about this – but Grandpa was the one to have the curse cast."

"The one to make sure none of Martina's family ever had kids..."

Before Ash could answer, another voice shouted from behind them, "Lies!"

Asher and Giselle jumped to their feet ready for a fight.

"Didn't I tell you to stay away from here?" An older man, maybe in his fifties, dirty blond hair with wisps of gray and a face full of beard, came strolling up from the other side of the creek. "Go on, get! This is my last warning, pups. Don't make me send you to your Alpha in a burlap sack."

"You wouldn't do it," Giselle surprised herself with her own boldness. It was a gamble, but one she felt she could win. This man had everything to do with this statue, and she wanted to get to the bottom of it.

"Little werewolf, don't tempt me." He looked like a vagabond straight off the panhandler's favorite overpass, and probably used this creek for bathing – which would explain why he smelled no different from the murky water. The smell of him should have alerted her or Asher long before he surprised her with his words, but that was not what worried her. The way he'd called Asher a liar... there was something more there.

"No one talks to me like that. I'll leave when I am good and ready, you hear me?" Giselle was shaken and worried, but she'd not let fear sound in her voice. Not with two male wolves around. She had to stand her ground and sound like she meant it, no matter what.

"I'll give you to the count of ten..." the old man said.

"You want me gone? You want me to never come

ain?" Giselle asked.

...One!"

"Then give me a better reason than a death threat."

"Two."

"How about answers?"

"Three."

"About this statue."

"Four."

"And the families here."

"Five."

"And the fact that you're connected to them." She was beginning to worry he'd make good on his threat, but she couldn't stop now.

"Six."

"Because you had a hand in it somehow."

"Seven."

"Because…" Shit… she didn't know what else to say. Her train of thought had derailed two numbers ago, and stalling wasn't helping matters.

"Eight."

"Ummm…" she looked at Asher, who seemed just as clueless as she was, but there was no hint of fear there. Alpha in the making, that one. Still, no help. Why wasn't he saying or doing anything?

"Nine."

And then, the lights flicked on behind Asher's eyes. "You're Jeffery Martins."

"How do you know that name, boy?" Jeffrey looked none too pleased to have been revealed.

"You're Christina's lover."

That got the old wolf's attention. "I am her only love. The one she was meant to marry, not that pompous, arrogant…"

That had Asher ready to strike. "Hey… that's my dad."

His whole body tensed, hands fisting, ready to pummel the old wolf. Giselle was a little more than annoyed that when they had been threatened, Asher had done nothing, but one mention of daddy, and he was up in arms. Hot boy or not, he was quickly losing points with her.

"I'm not sorry for stating the obvious," the old wolf said.

"You should be," Asher growled. Fur was beginning to darken on his skin. Giselle sensed he was struggling to keep his wolf at bay.

"Well, I'm not. Your father and the whole Thrace family can burn in hell, for all I care."

"Another fan, I see." Giselle gave a warning look at Asher to remind him why they were there. They needed this old wolf and for the truth to be told. Nothing would come from an unnecessary brawl, no matter who hated whom at this point. Whether Asher understood the cold narrowness of her eyes or not, she'd never know. But for his part, Asher remained where he was and held his tongue.

"Get off my property..." Jeffrey started to say, but Giselle cut him off.

"Not until I get answers. And besides, this is Martina's territory, not yours."

"Lippy pups like yourself find themselves at the wrong end of my teeth." He snapped his jaw at her. Probably more effective in his wolf form, but a threat just the same.

Giselle held her ground. "You like to threaten, don't you?" She met his eyes hard with the coldest stare she could muster. "What's your real issue here? You're not just a loner. You have no business out here in the middle of nowhere. Why are you protecting this place? Is it because of the wolf statue?"

The old wolf glanced just briefly over at Asher and then back to meet Giselle's dominant stare. "If you're planning on making this one your mate, you're in for trouble."

Giselle was taken aback, breaking eye contact to look ever so briefly at Asher. He too looked just as uncertain. "I'm taking no mate," she said.

"I was talking to the boy, who's clearly infatuated with you. He's not half the dominant you are, though." Jeffrey chuckled, and that eased the tension just slightly.

Not sure how to respond, Giselle locked eyes with the old wolf again, and tried to regain her anger. Dominance worked best when you had the power of rage behind it. "Are you going to tell me what I want to know?"

He sighed and turned toward the cave where the statue remained hidden. "Christina was Martina's sister... and my wife." He paused and let the weight of that revelation sink in.

"Christina was not married!" Asher blurted out.

"And you were alive when the marriage happened? Funny, I don't remember you on the guest list."

"My father—"

"Your father and her father were bullies. They forced my poor Christina into that arranged marriage. She never wanted to be part of the damn pack merger. Martina did, but your father wouldn't have her because she was barren. So my Christina was the only one suitable."

"Martina was already barren? But how did they know?" Giselle asked, remembering how talks of curses had started some of the infighting.

"Not my place to say, but Christina told me about the cancer and her operation." Jeffrey, despite the animosity, spoke respectfully about Martina's condition. "She'd never have kids."

"So she was no good for breeding?" Giselle was disgusted. If this was pack politics, it didn't matter who offered, she was never joining a pack.

"Correct. So Christina was only eligible Hernandez girl. It didn't matter that Christina and I were in love. We were ready to make our vows as mates, and she was forced into that stupid contract."

"So, what happened? She obviously didn't marry him."

"We married in secret, and when it came to light, she was the one who was punished."

"How?"

He pointed back to the cave. "You saw her. In the cave."

And that confirmed it. The statue looked so real because it was... a perfectly preserved wolf. A living breathing thing trapped in a tomb of stone.

"She's alive in there, isn't she?" Giselle asked.

"She is the stone."

"But how?"

"Magic. Old man Thrace paid a pretty penny to have this done to my Christina."

"My grandpa didn't do this," Asher said.

"He most certainly did. He wanted her life forfeit for the dishonor. And it was all her father could do to keep her from actually dying. They both agreed to this as punishment..."

"How could anyone agree to this?" Giselle wondered aloud.

"She's not dead." The old man said, "Though I bet if you could ask her, she'd like to be."

"So death or permanent prison in stone is punishment for marrying your true love... and you wonder why I don't rush to sign on as part of a pack?"

Asher laughed. "You were ready to before my warning."

"Neither of those packs is innocent. They both did this to Christina."

"Fair enough, but why did the war continue after the

fact? They made their peace with this… punishment, right?"

"Nah. Old man Thrace was never happy. Martina was offered as a second choice, a peace offering, but by then she'd too turned down the marriage and when retribution was threatened, war broke out again between the packs. Thrace had a witch in his pocket, and Martina had men to fight for her. No one fought cleanly, and many lives were lost."

"And what did you do? By marrying Christina, you should have been part of the pack," Asher pointed out. "Why did you not fight for your lady's honor?"

"Honor?" Jeffrey spat the word. "What does a pup like you know of honor? That war was not of my making, and I would no sooner fight for either side as both were guilty. Don't speak to me of honor. I did what I could for my love."

The pain mixed with rage in Jeffrey's voice threatened to bring tears to Giselle's eyes. She couldn't fathom the life he had led after the pain of losing Christina. And to have spent all those years here in the dry dusty desert with nothing… It was no wonder he was such an angry man. "So you just watched and waited?" she asked, trying to be sensitive to his pain, while still learning anything more that she could.

"I protected Christina. What else could I do?" He turned away and wiped his eyes, or maybe just his brow, Giselle couldn't quite tell. "Now, I've told you all you need to know. This is the last time I warn you. Come back here, and I will kill you both. I have no love for either of your packs."

"I belong to no pack." Giselle said.

"Yes, you do; you just haven't signed on the dotted line yet."

She sneered at the assumption. "I am my own wolf."

"For now. And only as long as you leave me alone. Understood?"

She'd hoped to learn more, but all the pain and sensitivity she'd heard in Jeffrey's voice had faded. Even his eyes had regained their icy sharpness. Learning all she could, Giselle conceded and shifted back into her wolf. She and Asher left in a slow jog back towards his truck.

25

She hadn't had much to say to Asher when they shifted back at his truck, nor did she take any extra time getting back to the house. The sun was blazing already, and Giselle wanted to make sure her outing had gone unnoticed. If even one person in that house got wind of her running off again, it would mean more problems. And she needed to process what she'd just learned before the drama it would create overwhelmed her.

Both packs were responsible. Both packs had been willing to sacrifice a young girl. And for what? A stupid marriage. What the hell century were they in that peace between reasonable people had to be sealed with a marriage vow?

If that was what pack life was all about, Giselle wanted to be counted out. She didn't care how nice the Hernandez family was, she wasn't signing on to any pack that would do that kind of crap.

Creeping in through the back gate, she made it to the kitchen before the sound of someone clearing their throat caught her off guard.

Gavin stepped out from behind the open refrigerator door. "Enjoy your run?"

She expected to meet with angry words or even a stern look, but Gavin's face was a neutral as could be, and that scared her even more. She almost wished to have found him in wolf form. Humans could mask their emotions far better than the wolf, and she needed a good read on Gavin.

"I wasn't alone." She knew better than to lie. And something about the honesty in their conversation the evening prior told her she could be truthful with him if anyone in this house.

"Thrace boy?"

How the hell did he know? "Yeah." No point in lying.

He stared at her silently for far longer than was comfortable. Still though, she couldn't gauge whether or not she was about to be in deep trouble or if he might just let this little infraction slide. When he finally did speak, the calm in his voice confirmed she'd be okay – this time. "He the reason you're conflicted?"

"One of them. I've got a witch who's getting friendly too." She winked, hoping she'd read the signals right.

Gavin cracked a smile, and his whole body relaxed. "Do yourself a favor. Play the field for a while before making any choices. Then settle down with a human."

Not what she'd expected, and certainly not the fatherly type of advice either, but she'd take it if it meant she wasn't grounded or worse for sneaking out again. "Sounds like you've got no love lost on either side."

"You're far too young to deal with the level of drama our kind bring. Keep it simple while you've still got your training wheels on."

She snorted at his phrasing but more so at the fact that it was just that – supernatural drama – that had her all conflicted. Too little, too late on that advice. "I'll keep that in mind. You won't tell, will you?"

He quirked an eyebrow at her and stood silent for a few

moments. "If you want to wash the smell of desert off you before the girls get up, you'd best go now."

She hoped that meant he'd keep her secret, but didn't want to test his patience by asking for confirmation, so she turned and headed towards the stairs.

"One more thing," Gavin said.

Giselle turned on the spot. "Yeah?"

"If you ever get an idea to sneak out with that Thrace boy again…"

Uh-oh… here it comes. She gulped, waiting for the hammer to drop.

"Leave a note, so someone knows where you are."

Again… not what she'd expected, but she'd take it. "Yeah. Sure."

"Not 'sure'… Yes!" There was no mistaking the order. He might have been easygoing about everything else, but on this she knew he would accept no mistakes.

"Yes. I will," she said, and meant it.

"Good." The calm returned to his voice, and she resumed heading up the stairs.

26

She hadn't intended on giving Asher the cold shoulder through Chemistry or even when he'd mentioned maybe discussing things over lunch. Giselle was still processing what she'd learned and the extent of what both packs had done to each other in the name of pack business. Death, betrayal, broken families. Seemed so medieval and archaic for such modern people to act that way.

But with that new knowledge came hope. If the current heads of family could see the result of their parents' treachery and fix what was done, maybe there was a chance for peace. And that meant she needed her witchy friend to give her some good news.

She rushed into Lit class a few minutes before the bell hoping to find Damien, and sure enough, he was there, snacking on some crackers at his desk, reading a comic book, looking just as adorable as ever.

She slid into her chair with all the smoothness of a wrecking ball. "I'm so glad to catch you now."

"You can't just chat me up when you want something, you know that?" Damien was all smiles when he said it, but Giselle picked up the note of tension and felt instantly embarrassed. She'd totally meant to talk with him after their fun trip up the mountain, but everything else had piled up on top of her. All she'd managed to do in the last few days was send a couple of quick one-liner texts.

Even when she wasn't trying, she managed to screw things up. She'd have written off a guy if he'd been so standoffish after a date... not that the trip up the mountains was a date. Or was it? Damn. Her head was all messed up. "I'm not, seriously. I know that sounds like a cop out, but it's the truth."

"Really?" His eyebrow jutted upwards in a very unbelieving way. "You've been quiet this week."

She deserved that. He was more than reasonable with his anger; although even when angry, Damien's eyes were melting her soul. "I know. I'm so sorry. I have been trying to catch up since I've missed so much class. And..."

"Spending time with him?" Damien pointed to Asher, taking his seat in the front row.

Now that was a low blow, and she was not about to let him get away with it. "He's part of the equation. And because of him, I know more information now."

Damien looked away and sighed.

Men. Boys, really. What the hell? She could expect pouting like that from Taylor or even Di. Not that she thought Di ever really pouted, but to see a guy do it... He had to be playing. All part of the game, right?

"Don't do that. It doesn't suit you!" She sharpened her tone.

He sighed again and made a visible effort to rein in his disappointment. "I'm not good at sharing, that's all."

Now it was her turn to give him the 'what the hell' look. "Who says you're sharing anything?"

"I'm not?"

"Uh... no... you're in competition," she said with a

wink.

"In that case, I'd better step up my game." Light found those gorgeous eyes of his, and he gave her a mischievous little nod.

That was more like it. She preferred the confident and self-assured version of Damien to the poor sport he had been playing at. Though she truly suspected that had been an act, especially as quickly as he turned it all around. "Well, I won't complain about that."

"Though I have to say, my news may put me in a bad light. I'd hate to lose the game so early on with failure."

Her interest was piqued. News? Failure? "What did you learn? I'll tell you mine if you tell me yours…" She tried to keep it light, but her voice betrayed her.

"That just sounds dirty."

"Hardly." Though she had hoped it would sound better than anxious. Her heart was racing. Surely Asher in the front of the class could hear it. She quickly glanced in his direction. If he had heard anything, he wasn't letting on. He sat drumming his pencil on his notepad, staring off at the blackboard or possibly just into space.

"How about you go first?" Damien said to her, snapping her attention back at him.

She leaned over, whispering so only they could hear, "The spell was ordered by both families. And the husband of Christina is still alive and well and protecting her in a cave not far from my pack's home."

"Interesting. A decision made by both caused the war. And you want to rescind it?"

"Yeah," she scoffed. "It didn't serve its purpose. Obviously. And that poor girl paid the price."

He nodded thoughtfully and sat back against the chair.

Anxiety swelled within her. Why wasn't he just coming out and saying what his mysterious failure was? The first bell rang and the class started filling up with people. Mrs. Freeman went to the blackboard and began writing questions for a pop quiz.

"Everyone please take out a sheet of paper, and answer the following. No books, please." She didn't look back to see who listened, she just kept on scrawling away with her lovely loopy writing.

Giselle leaned over with the pretense of grabbing a pencil from her bag. "Well?" she said impatiently.

"Well, that brings us to the bad news. I'm afraid the particular spell in question can only be undone by the person who cast it."

"Oooh… That's tricky." And would complicate matters much more than she'd anticipated. Nothing could ever just be simple, could it? "So, what do we do?"

Mrs. Freeman cleared her throat. "No talking, class!"

Giselle growled under her breath and glared at her teacher's back. She just needed five more minutes to clear the air. Was that too much to ask?

Damien whispered low. "Doctor-patient confidentially means no one will own up to it."

"Damn. Dead end." She cracked the pencil in her hand, not realizing how hard she'd been holding it.

Concern flashed in Damien's eyes. "Sorry. I didn't mean to put such a final note on it."

Her mood had turned foul, and to top it off, she hadn't caught up on the reading, and by the look of the questions on the board, she was not going to do well on this test either. Things were going from bad to worse, and her heart had already been racing before his bad news. Now it threatened to give up, as she saw the utter futility of her attempt to fix the situation. Her wolf, sensing her anxiety, gnawed at her from within, begging to be allowed a chance to surface and take care of whatever was causing her stress.

Breathe. Just Breathe, she told herself. Remembering her breathing and centering herself in the moment. That always helped. There might be other ways to work on things. But for now, she had to breathe and calm down.

Damien whispered, lower this time, "You okay?"

"Fine." She was able to calm her wolf for the moment and send her back down, but anxiety still threatened to take over.

"When a girl says she's fine, she's anything but…"

"I'm okay. Just… okay." She really didn't have anything else to add at that point. "After school. Let's talk."

"How about pizza tonight?"

His invitation caught her off guard, in a good way. "You never miss an opportunity, do you?"

"Not when I'm in competition." He winked, and whether it was that gesture or the fact that his eyes were irresistible, it helped melt more of her tension. She was able to breathe a little easier.

"Ms. Richards. Mr. Matthews. If I have to remind you two again to be quiet, you will take an F on today's assignment."

"Sorry, Mrs. Freeman." Damn. She just couldn't avoid getting in trouble at school. Maybe Gavin had been right – supernatural drama was too much for high school. She lowered her head and tried as hard as she could to keep quiet and answer the questions.

27

Giselle hunkered down in the bedroom, headphones on, trying to catch up on her homework so she'd have time to meet Damien for pizza. She hardly noticed Di and Taylor come in, or the fact they'd brought peace offerings.

"You've been awfully mysterious lately." Di tapped Giselle on the shoulder.

She jumped from surprise, hitting her head on the top bunk. "Ouch. Damn. Warn a girl!"

"We thought" – Taylor pointed to herself and Di – "that we'd been a bit cold about the whole joining the pack thing, and wanted to make up."

"We're fine. Really," Giselle said. "But I'll take the donut anyway."

"I don't pretend to know what's going on, but I know you're hiding something, and we've said before we want to help." Taylor offered a chocolate-covered crème filled donut, holding it like a treat but not handing it over just yet. "But you have to trust us."

Giselle snatched the tasty pastry and took a bite before Taylor could try to retrieve it. "I'm not a dog. You can't buy me with treats." She laughed. "But if you keep the donuts coming, I might learn to fetch and play dead."

Di snickered. "Keep going into the desert alone and you might…"

"Speaking of that." Taylor fixed her with a stone-cold 'I know what you did last night' gaze.

"Yeah. I did. Early this morning." Giselle looked defiantly at both girls. She wasn't under their rule and had no reason to fear any retribution, especially since Gavin had already busted her and given her a reprieve.

"Thought so," Taylor said. "Asher didn't leave you hanging this time, did he?"

"He did what?" The shock in Di's voice surprised Giselle.

"No. He didn't leave this time, and I got more answers and more problems to solve at the same time." Giselle sighed. She set her books aside and reached for the box of donuts again.

"I'm afraid that's all you'll ever find." Taylor sounded so resigned. It wasn't like her. She was always the perky, 'I can make it work' type.

Giselle wondered how much of her new information to divulge. Taylor would have her back, no question, but Di had always made it seem like she was one screw-up away from being sent back to the girl's home. They were both to be her sisters if it all worked out, and that tipped the scales in their favor. Giselle only hoped that rehashing all the bullshit would give her answers rather than more problems, especially after what Damien had said about witchy law.

"Here's the thing," she said, snatching yet another pastry. "Both families are screwed up. And both families are to blame for this stupid war."

"Yeah, but what are you going to do about it? You can't change their minds. You're just some loner pup." Di's attitude made Giselle instantly regretful she'd opened her mouth. *Loner pup.* Those words shouldn't have bothered her as much as they did, but just hearing them had her wolf's attention.

"I mean, I'm sure you mean well." Had Di caught the flash of wolf in her eyes? Di's tone changed with breakneck speed. "We all want peace, but what can any of us kids do?"

Giselle took a calming breath and a bite of her donut before responding. "What if I told you I could do something… or I *might* be able to. But I have to figure out how."

"I don't think you can, and you need to stop this. Either join up, or reject the offer – and when you're eighteen you can walk away with no ties." And Di was right back on Giselle's shit list. Her attitude was like nails on a chalkboard. But rather than rise to the veiled taunting, Giselle controlled her urge to smack the blonde girl and opt for peace. Since that was, after all, what she was after. Peace.

"I like you guys. Even you, Di. I can't let this go now that I've learned so much. I think I might have found Christina!"

That got the girls' attention. Everyone had assumed she was dead, so the possibilities of that being false had all kinds of potential.

"So, what kind of help do you need?" Taylor asked, more than eager now to assist.

Popping the last of her donut into her mouth she debated whether or not to have another. Pizza was soon, and she really should ease up on the junk food, even if her wolf was begging for it. "I'm going to talk to Damien tonight. He asked me out to Sammy's for pizza. I think I know where Christina is, but before I take things further, I need magical mumbo-jumbo. Maybe he can give me some answers."

"I know I said Damien was preferable to Ash, but don't get involved with a witch. They can be tricky people. And never get into a contract with them…" Di's warning sounded too cautious.

"Why? What do you know about him that you're not saying?" Giselle asked.

"Nothing." Di looked away, embarrassment coloring her cheeks. Whatever those two had done in the past must have been really interesting, but neither of them was talking. Damn that doctor-patient confidentiality crap. Someone would have to speak up sooner or later.

"You had him do a spell for you, didn't you?" Giselle asked, hoping she'd get it out of Di first.

"It was nothing, really." All evidence to the contrary, Di was shielding her eyes now too. It must have been good.

"Doctor-patient confidentiality?" Giselle asked.

Di nodded. "Goes both ways. I can't talk either."

"Not fair. Sisters shouldn't have secrets." Giselle hoped playing up that angle would help, but Di wasn't budging. She even made a zipper motion across her lips for effect. Damn it!

Taylor looked at Di, shocked. "What did you have him do for you?" Apparently, sisters did have secrets.

Di looked as if she were about to burst. "Nothing too bad, okay? Drop it. All I can say is... magical contract."

Giselle's stomach sank; she was just about to tell the girls the plan and remembered the handshake with Damien. The strange vibration. Had that really been a magical contract? What would be the consequences? She had to hold her tongue before saying anything more.

Di picked up a magazine and hid her face behind it. "I'm just saying, Elle, be careful with witches."

Giselle hadn't though about any dangers in being involved, even on a friendly level, with a witch, but seeing how closed off Di was about the subject gave her a little bit of worry. Damien seemed so nice, though. He couldn't possibly be more of a problem than Asher had been, right?

"I'm just going to ask him what he knows, that's all. No magical funny business."

"Want us to go with you?" Taylor asked.

"No. But I'll tell you what I find out from him. As for Asher, we took that run and found the loner guarding a wolf statue... I think it might be Christina."

Taylor's eyes lit up. "If it is... Martina—"

Giselle cut her off. "—will need to find out after we figure out what can be done about it. No good in telling her beforehand."

Excitement faded from Taylor's eyes. "Okay," she said with all the disappointment of a girl who'd just been told the Easter bunny wasn't real.

Diana, on the other hand, regained her sharp tone. She lowered the magazine and fixed Giselle with a warning glare. "She might be best never knowing her sister may be a statue. She lives with the hope she'll one day find her – to show her the finality of it would be crushing."

Di and Giselle might go round and round on many things, but Di's love for Martina was something Giselle never questioned. It had been the only thing that made Giselle trust in Diana. For all the attitude and posturing, the pretty princes had a true loyal heart where family was concerned. That was worth the petty infighting. "And that's why we say nothing until we have all the facts," Giselle agreed.

"And you think Damien is going to have some facts?" Taylor asked.

"Never said that. Just that I want to look at all pieces of the puzzle."

"And he's a fine piece to look at." Taylor giggled.

Di slapped her shoulder. "Tay!"

"What? I've always thought he was hot, but he's never looked my way." She shrugged. "I think he likes redheads."

"He likes blondes too," Di said defensively.

"He seems like a flirt, no matter what the hair," Giselle said. "But an honest one. If my wolfy senses are correct."

Di shrugged. "He's not evil. I'll say that, but he's no pure soul."

"Just let me go out tonight, alone, and see what I can dig up. Maybe I come home with more than just leftovers…"

"What's that supposed to mean?" Di screwed up her face in confusion.

Giselle sighed impatiently. "I mean information. Something we can use to help clear the air."

"Keep dreaming, sister," Di said.

"I will." Giselle stuck out her tongue.

"Well, whatever…" Taylor stood and walked to the closet. "You're not leaving the house in that."

28

"Okay, so when you said pizza, honestly I was thinking the cheapo five-dollar variety, not a sit down restaurant." Giselle suddenly felt so thankful for her fashionista sister-person. Taylor had picked out the maxi dress with dark jean jacket combo for her instead of the jeans and t-shirt she'd planned on. Much more appropriate for the date-ish setting they were in.

"They have the best pizza here. Wood-fired and made with real toppings." Damien looked around for the waiter and waved him over.

"Welcome to Sammy's. Would you like some drinks to start?"

Even the waiter looked five-star, Giselle thought. Black outfit with a pristine white apron and gold name tag. Steve was his name, and he smiled down at the table, looking at Giselle first to take an order. Too bad she hadn't studied the menu yet. And somehow, ordering a soda felt a little too low class. Maybe an Arnold Palmer would be more appropriate, but who wanted tea with pizza?

"Tea for me and…." Damien waved to Giselle.

Crap, she had to decide already. Oh, well, tea it was.

"The same, thanks."

"Passion fruit okay?"

"Uh… sure." Giselle was having a hard time regaining her focus. She really hadn't intended on a date. Just a 'get to know you' kind of chat over a greasy slice of unhealthy goodness.

"Did I go over the top? You look like a scared rabbit."

Giselle laughed. She could eat a rabbit right about now. Her wolf was as anxious as she, and a nice unhealthy meal with lots of meat would help settle that nicely. "No. Sorry. Just, you know… processing."

"I like you." He locked her into his irresistible gaze.

"Really? I couldn't tell," she smirked, hoping that sounded funny rather than snarky. She'd been having so hard a time managing not to sound bitchy around him. "But I thought that was common knowledge."

"It is; but *why* isn't."

"Okay, why?"

"You're unfiltered. You say what's out there and don't hold back. You stand up for your convictions."

"And you got all that from knowing me for a week?"

"Yeah," he said, with no hint of irony.

She had a quick-fire response at the ready, but paused, wondering if she needed to say anything at all. He seemed to be reading her quite accurately.

He leaned in across the table. "The fact you want what's best for all, not just for yourself, is refreshing. Not something most teens do. And certainly not what the wolves in this town do."

She was definitely getting that last part. The stupidity of the whole pack war was over the top. How could modern people be so archaic? And maybe not having grown up in a pack was a good thing for her, or she might have been one of those who followed mindlessly into battle.

"What about you?" She turned the question round on him. "Would you do what's best for all or yourself?"

"All for one, and that one is me. I'll freely admit I am selfish…. in a good way."

She laughed at his truth, because she shared some of the sentiment. "My intentions are pretty selfish too. I won't align myself with a family at war. I don't see the point in signing up for a fight I didn't start."

"See? Honesty. Raw and unfiltered."

She sighed. "But honesty doesn't solve anything at this point."

"It might."

"I thought about what was said earlier. I can't make anyone 'fess up to the spell, but they can undo it."

Giselle nodded. "If they were willing?"

"Right. They'd have to be willing, which means I'd have to do some talking."

"Me too. The girls want to help, but don't know how."

"So, let's drop the rule of silence and figure out a way to bring everyone to the same conclusion: that this statue should be returned to its original form."

"You mean I can speak freely to the girls?"

"Yeah, and I can speak freely to my family. Of course, when I do, they will probably take an interest in you."

"What does that mean?"

"Unclaimed wolf in town. Witches always make it a point to know what's going on around them. It helps keep us protected."

"But that doesn't tell me what kind of interest they will take."

"I don't exactly know. Just that you'll be on their radar. There will always be eyes out. Be aware of it, whatever you do."

"That sounds pretty scary."

He shrugged. "We know wolf business. We know vampire business. All supernatural business is our business."

"You sound like the mob."

She'd said it in jest, but the look on his face confirmed she'd actually hit the nail on the head, dead on.

"Okay, so we discuss amongst our people, and then what?"

The waiter returned with their drinks and, noticing they were deep in conversation, left without taking their order. Damn... he was good. Giselle made a note to leave a good tip.

Behind her, Giselle heard the door open. That would not have normally piqued her interest, except for the smell that wafted in with it: wolf.

She turned to see Asher walking in. Their eyes locked, and surprisingly, he strolled over.

Coldness washed over Damien's features, but he kept his tone light. "Everyone likes Sammy's. I told you it was the best."

"So I see." Giselle smiled at Asher.

"Can I join you for a moment?"

"Are you stalking me?" she asked.

"We're kind of having a..." Damien tried to say, but Asher scooted onto the bench next to Giselle.

"I've heard things, and I want to talk to both of you about them." His tone brooked no argument. "Before my father gets here."

Giselle was caught completely off guard, and sat there with two of the cutest boys she'd ever met... was it hot in there or was it just them? Damn...

Damien's heat came from simmering anger at that moment. He looked moments away from a fight with the wolf, and Giselle guessed only the public setting was saving them all from a brawl. Gritting his teeth to keep his face as neutral as he could, he took in slow breaths before speaking. "What do you want, wolf?"

If Asher was bothered by the way Damien spoke to him, it didn't show. Maybe he was too self-assured in his abilities, or maybe he didn't see Damien as any real threat. Either way, his tone was completely opposite of the witch's. "You know Giselle and I found something. Something that may change the course of our families."

"Yes, we were discussing that – alone."

Again, Asher ignored Damien's tone. "I have an idea."

"Go on," Giselle said.

"The full moon is soon. We'll all be out. Why not find a way for us all to be out together?"

"The wolf packs... both of them... in one place, during a full moon... ludicrous! Are you trying to get everyone killed?"

"I think it would do good. Giselle and I can bring both packs to the cave. Damien, your people will be setting up the moon rituals... make them do it at the cave. Find a reason for them to be there."

"What about the lone wolf?" Giselle asked. "Jeffrey was quite clear he wanted to be left alone."

"You and I will go back to him and explain what we plan to do," Asher said. "He trusts you."

"Barely. He wants us dead if we trespass again."

"Not if we make him understand he'll get his wife back." Asher's tone was as Alpha as it got. He meant business, and Giselle wondered if she'd judged him poorly before. He was clearly trying to make things right, even if he was a bit pushy about it.

"You're both insane if you think an asinine plan like this would ever work," Damien said.

Ash looked down at Giselle. Their eyes met, and despite Giselle's apprehension, her resolve melted.

"Let's try," she said, feeling keener than before about Asher's prospects. He might be a bit brutish, but he had a heart underneath that aloof exterior.

Damien huffed loudly.

"You have a better plan?" Asher turned on him, and there was more than just annoyance in his voice.

"No, but collecting two families at war against each other, together with a lone wolf with a grudge, and a powerful witch coven in one place during the moon…" Damien threw up his hands in frustration. "World War Three would be less catastrophic."

"Do be dramatic!" Giselle said.

Both boys turned on her with shock etched across their faces.

"Damien has a point. Don't act as if this will be easy," Asher said.

"Well, it's the best plan we've got, so I'm going to attempt to stay positive," Giselle said.

The waiter returned and asked for their orders.

"He's not staying…" Damien fixed Asher with a surprisingly Alpha-worthy glare.

"No. I'm not. But we'll be in touch." Asher took his leave, walking a few tables over and setting himself down.

The door opened again and the smell of wolf intensified. Giselle resisted the temptation to turn around, instead waiting for whoever it was to walk past. And he did. A tall male, one built like a personal trainer, too. He joined Asher at the table ahead of theirs and the two began to talk.

"Order whatever," Giselle said trying to get a good look at the other wolf – Asher's father if she wasn't mistaken – without getting caught. "Surprise me with the best pizza in town."

"You want the anchovy special?" Damien asked, but Giselle failed to pick up the note of annoyance in his voice.

"Yeah… go for it." She nodded, watching Asher and his father engaged in conversation.

Damien must have ordered because when she finally looked his direction, she found him oddly upset.

"Nothing will change, you know." His choice of words was odd, but it was the finality in his voice that confused her most. What exactly was it he thought wouldn't change? "If the packs could stop fighting, that would be enough for me."

"So you can…"

She cut him off before his jealousy could finish that sentence. "…have a family with no baggage."

"All families have baggage."

"True, but most of their baggage won't kill you. Just send you though years of therapy, if you're lucky."

The joke seemed to be lost on Damien, but then he lightened up. "So you've met my family then?" He laughed, and the ugly jealousy faded.

Her eyes wandered back over to Asher's table. He and his father were engaged in such a friendly looking discussion. Father-son bonding time or something. She'd never seen Asher look so… was that pride? Gone was the stony wall he held up at school. Here he was easygoing, and dare she think it… happy. How could Mr. Thrace be that bad, when seeing him with his son he appeared the doting dad? "I want to talk to him."

"What? Are you insane?"

"He doesn't look so mean." Really, he didn't. He had the same handsome features that Asher had obviously inherited. The strong jaw, dark hair, with just a hint of five o'clock shadow, and a toothy grin that almost welcomed her over without words. "I'm going to say hi."

"Don't…" Damien's words fell on deaf ears.

Giselle was already up and walking over. "Hey, Ash,"

she called out ahead of her.

His head popped up a moment before his father's. The happy-go-lucky expression faded into one of warning. It was too late, though – she'd already spoken, already drawn attention to herself... No going back. "Just wanted to say hi. I never met your dad. It's so nice to meet..."

"Are you a new waitress here?" Mr. Thrace speared her with his cold eyes and practically barked at her.

Her voice faltered. "No... why?"

"Were you invited to dine with us?"

"No. I just saw Ash, and—"

"You just thought you'd barge in on my time with my son."

"No. Sorry. I was just..."

"A rude little girl who doesn't know her place." His nostrils flared, no doubt picking up her wolfy smell, if he hadn't already, and his eye twitched with the strain of someone struggling very hard to remain civil. "You smell familiar." He took a long slow inhale. "Yes. I've smelled your stench before."

She cringed at the word 'stench.' How dare he!

"You've been around my home. In my kitchen and pantry. No doubt my son has had you. Savor whatever moments he gave you, as your kind are not worth wasting much time on – but do not think yourself equal to us, and do not stand here gawking any longer."

Shock stole the sound from her voice, but inner rage had her mind running a mile a minute with what she'd love to say to that man. "You see here, sir. I was just coming over to politely introduce myself. I'm a classmate of your son. An equal, though you seem to not understand the concept. He's a friend, and if anyone is being rude here, it's you." She'd meant to say all that, but the words had not actually left her mouth; they'd stuck themselves somewhere near the back, refusing to come out against the dangerous Alpha-wolf staring her down. Even her own wolf, who usually begged for a chance to rise and fight, was keeping quiet.

Ash came to her rescue after she'd stood mouth agape for far too long to not be awkward. "She's fine, dad. Just a friend. But Giselle, let's talk later. Okay?"

Still unable to muster the words, she just nodded and turned away.

"That looked painful."

If Damien had laughed at her she might have unleashed her wolf then and there she was raging so hard, but thankfully, his words were sympathetic. Still, she needed some time to cool down and find her voice. She could see now why people thought he was a jerk. He was!

"I'd tell you to relax, but I know that's not going to happen." He glared over at Ash's table and then looked back at Giselle. "Everyone knows he's a jerk."

She let out a deep breath. He was a jerk, but why? Unchecked aggression like that. There had to be something else there. Maybe he'd smelled wolf and that set him off. He was an Alpha, and she was unknown. Angry as she was, after a moment to cool off, she realized she could have approached it better. Not that it gave Mr. Thrace an excuse to be an outright ass, but for her part, she could have saved herself some embarrassment.

"I'm fine." She finally found her voice.

"Yeah, you are," Damien returned with a refreshingly flirty smile.

That made her giggle and release some of the pent-up tension. "Thanks. I needed that."

"You looked like you were about to wolf out there, for a moment."

"I was. Had to calm down, that's all."

"Do you want to go? We can make this take out and find a little park close by."

"Aren't you the romantic?"

"I try."

"Nah. We can't leave now."

He did a double take over to Ash's table and back at theirs. "No one's looking. Quick, you go out the back."

"It's a wolf thing. If I leave now, he's won."

"Ahhh. So it's a pride thing."

"Sure. Go with that." It was close enough to the truth. And also, she really was hungry, and the smell of pizza was much more tempting than licking her wounds.

Damien shrugged. "Have it your way then."

"Speaking of that… what exactly did you order? Not anchovies, right?"

"So you were listening?"

"You have got to get over the jealousy thing."

"Not jealous. Never jealous. Okay… maybe a little jealous. You are supposed to be out with me tonight… remember?"

"I am. And you have my full attention."

"Liar. Don't make me use witchy funny business to force the truth out of you."

"You'd never…"

"Don't tempt me."

She narrowed her eyes at him like she was ready to pounce.

"Okay. Okay… don't hurt me. You're really cute when you get all predator, you know."

She giggled. "Bet you say that to all the wolves."

"Nah. Just you… and Di…. And Taylor." He listed them on his finger.

"Thought you didn't have a thing for Di?"

"Nah, just…" he stopped himself.

"Doctor-patient confidentiality."

"Yep."

"C'mon… you have to tell me at least something."

"I can't tell you. I can't even give you clues as to what I did to work with Di."

"Well, you're just no fun."

"Sorry, that's how the game is played. Some rules just can't be broken for any reason."

She relaxed back into the booth and nodded. As much as she hated it, it was a really good thing he could keep a secret. That made him more than trustworthy.

"And now we hit the awkward silence phase of our date."

Giselle was practically bursting with laughter, the bubbly sort of mini-explosions that only comes from true amusement. Damien was so easy to like, always finding a way to twist the situation and find just the right note of humor. He matched her smile with his own and reached out across the table to grab her hand. Rather than pull away, as would have been her instinct, she allowed it, embracing the warmth of his touch and even enjoying the connection to another human being. After another silent but definitely not awkward moment of them just sitting and holding hands, Damien leaned in and whispered, "I ordered meat lover's pizza."

Damn. He was a keeper!

29

"So… how'd it go?" Taylor met her at the door, pulling her inside before she could get the key out of the lock. "I want every juicy detail."

She should have expected it, but Taylor's enthusiasm was almost overwhelming. She'd hardly stepped one foot in the door before her new sister was slamming it shut and standing against it as if to hold her hostage for the information.

"It was fine, except for the part where Mr. Thrace told me I was worthless."

Taylor's eyes grew three sizes, or so it seemed that moment, and her jaw nearly hit the floor. "He did what?"

"Apparently Ash and his dad were having dinner at the same place as us. I went to say hi and left with my tail tucked between my legs."

"He's a jerk."

"That's the understatement of the century." Giselle yawned and walked to the kitchen to put her pizza box in the fridge. "He is every bit as mean as you all said."

"See now why you shouldn't believe what Ash is saying about our pack?"

"The thing is, Ash never really talked crap about us. He just warned me about the pack war."

"You did it!" Taylor squealed.

"Did what now?"

"You said *us*... as in all of us. As in pack."

She had, hadn't she? It might not be official, but even with all the animosity in the air, she was beginning to feel like they really were her pack mates, and at least Taylor felt like a sister.

"Don't get cocky..." She tried to sound a warning but Taylor's look said she wasn't convinced.

"So how did Damien take all of this? I mean, he knows you're sweet on Ash, and he was there trying to be all studly with you. "

"Oh, he was great... even ordered meat lover's pizza."

"Awww. Be still my heart, he ordered you pizza." Taylor giggled.

"Shut up." She playfully smacked Tay's shoulder. "It was nice."

"I'll bet. And did you share a slice all romantic-like?"

Giselle's face flushed, but not because she'd been caught being a girl. She was a girl. But Taylor was painting a picture of some romantic dinner Lady and the Tramp style, when truth was, she'd wolfed down her pizza like the wild animal she was. He'd even ordered a second one to help sate her hunger. Damn the full moon.

"You kissed, didn't you?" Taylor looked shocked.

"No. We held hands, and talked." And that was more than she had really been prepared for. It had been nice, very nice, but dating was a whole new world to navigate. Especially dating in the supernatural world.

"Look at you, all flustered. You and Damien really hit it off." Taylor was smiling ear to ear, but Giselle detected a tiny hint of jealousy there.

"Stop. Really. We have more important things to deal with right now. Let's talk about the wolf statue…" Anything to change the subject.

Her smile faded. "Fine. Be that way, but I need to live vicariously thorough someone's love life."

"Why? Don't you have men knocking down the door for you?"

"Boys… yes, but no one I really want to date."

"That's a big problem." Sarcasm didn't seem to work on Taylor.

"It is when the boy you like is crushing on other girls." Taylor's tone said more than Giselle wanted to hear. Now she felt bad for going out with Damien.

"You mean Damien, don't you?"

"No. Not him. He's not my type." She shrugged, but that wasn't convincing anyone.

"Liar."

"Whatever." Taylor had never looked so flustered.

"Do you really like him?"

"No. I'm just a little…"

"Jealous?"

"You've been at school all of two weeks and have two of the hottest boys in school talking to you. I've been class president, prom committee, and countless other social club advisors, and those two have never set eyes on me."

"I doubt it has anything to do with looks or social standing… They're not prom committee type of guys."

"I'm also a cheerleader."

"And Damien is no jock… and Asher hates this family." She was struggling to make a good defense but failing miserably, and Taylor's watery eyes made things so much worse.

"Look. I'm happy for you. I am…" Taylor looked like she wanted to cry.

"Do you want me to stop talking to Damien? Or maybe tell him you think he's cute?"

"No. God, no! Nothing like that."

"Then what?"

"Just… be good to him."

That was the last thing she'd expected Taylor to say.

"Yeah. Sure. Of course. But I'm not even seriously…"

"Just drop it. Be good. That's all." She wiped her face, brushing away tears and the smudge of mascara.

Giselle was no good at feelings, especially others' feelings. Should she try to hug Taylor, or would that make things worse? Crap. What to do? Change the subject. "Okay… moving on. Tomorrow night. We're going to run the pack to the creek."

"Martina won't go for that."

"We have to. It's our only hope. Ash and Damien will bring their groups, and we can all air out our grievances together."

The shock of her plan seemed to pull the emotion from Taylor's eyes. "Or start an all-out war."

"That too, but we have to do something. All three families are tied together, and the wolf statue is the key!"

"You're insane. It will never work."

"It has to."

"We're all going to die." Taylor looked as if boys were now the last thing on her mind. At least Giselle had managed to fix that problem.

"That's the spirit!"

"No. Seriously. You're going to get us all killed."

"To be honest… I don't agree. You said you'd help, so will you?"

"I don't know how you plan to pull it off, but I'll keep my word."

Giselle hoped she was right in thinking once everyone

saw the statue, they'd find a way to talk rather than fight, but it was a huge gamble. She gulped down the apprehension she was feeling and put on a brave face. "Thank you!"

30

The day of the full moon arrived, and Giselle was itching to get out and run. She couldn't wait to confirm their plans with Asher. She scooted into class a few minutes early and practically pounced on the sleepy-eyed wolf when he lumbered into the room.

"I'm going to bring the pack to the cave tonight. What time do you think you'll have your people there, and how many of your pack will be coming?"

"Not tonight, okay." He yawned and tossed his bag on the table.

She did have her days right, right? It was the full moon, wasn't it? She could feel the pull already. Maybe he'd forgotten what day it was. "Um... hello? This was your idea. And it's full moon tonight. We agreed we needed to try and do it now."

He flopped into his seat and opened up his notebook to the wolf picture he'd been working on. It had taken up the entire notebook page now, with intricately patterned trees and hidden images of other wolves looking down on the central one baying at the full moon. "We agreed to get everyone in the same place to bring out the truth." He yawned again – more like roared by the sound of it. Was he a lion or a wolf?

"Did you wake up in another time zone or something? When better than a full moon to get the groups together?"

"Not tonight, okay? Wait until next month."

She stifled her own frustrated growl. "Why?"

"Last night's meeting didn't go too well."

"Yeah, your dad's a dick!"

His head snapped in her direction. "He's my father."

"I'm sorry… for that."

His lip twitched, and she could have sworn she saw his teeth sharpening beneath.

That didn't stop her, though, from continuing. "Being old and an Alpha does not give anyone the right to act like he did. If you're defending his actions, you're no better."

Asher's breath slowed, deliberately taking in long pulls of air and audibly letting them out. "I do not have control over his actions, but if you wish this idea to have any chance, you need to let me smooth the way. He's not going to listen to anything right now, agitated as he is."

"And what does the great Alpha have to be agitated about?" She should have let it drop, but couldn't hold her tongue.

"Some hot head young lone wolf sticking her nose where it doesn't belong."

If she hadn't been in class with other normal people nearby and a teacher who was already out to get her, she might have risen to his challenge and snapped at him. But she forced herself to take the high road, and after a moment of silence to calm her inner wolf, she said, "I'll be there, whether you are or not."

"What is that supposed to mean?"

"Exactly what I said."

"But the old loner?"

"Will kill trespassers... yes, I heard the threat."

"You won't go. You won't subject your pack to possible slaughter."

"First of all, they're not my pack... yet. And second, who says they'd get slaughtered? He's only one wolf."

"Your pack has two feeble adults and three pups...need I say more?"

They might not have been her pack officially, and she might not have known them for very long, but loyalty had already taken root with her, and his insult would not stand. Whatever forgiveness for his attitude she'd given him before no longer applied. He was just as much a dick as his father. How dare he! "You know what? We're done here..."

"I didn't mean..."

"No. Stop. We're done."

"Giselle..."

She raised her hand and got the attention of Mr. Harper. "I'm going to need a new lab partner."

"Having another lover's quarrel, Ms. Richards?" Mr. Harper must have enjoyed embarrassing her. The smile on his face was proof enough of that.

"Sure. Whatever. I can't work with him."

"Ms. Richards, in life and in this classroom, we all have to work with people we don't like. Suck it up." He turned his back on her and began scrawling out instructions for the day's experiment on the board.

So much for her grand exit.

"You're stuck with me, so let's forget I said that. I'm sorry." Asher was trying, but Giselle wasn't taking it.

"I said, we're done. And you can do whatever the hell you want with the full moon. I don't need you." All she really needed was to show Martina that her sister was alive, and as long as Damien was still on her side and could get his people there, it should still work out.

31

After lunch she met Damien in class, hoping he had better news for her than Asher had. That jerkoff of a wolf's attitude had left a sour taste in her mouth.

"Ready for tonight?" she asked, sliding into her chair.

Damien smiled as usual, but something was missing. "'Ready' is not the word."

"What is that supposed to mean?"

"Well, I'm not a coven elder or even a leader, so no one really listens to me when I ask for things."

"So that means…" All the air left her chest. This plan had been doomed to fail from the start, and now both Ash and Damien were confirming the futility. Why bother, right?

"Don't look so sad… We're not dead in the water yet."

"Yet… Ash doesn't care. He won't be there. And now you…"

"Wait, Ash backed out? Why?"

"Blames his father's grumpiness on me."

"That's a lie."

"And how do you know?"

"A little lone wolf wouldn't cause so much trouble. Something else has to be going on."

"Whatever it is, Ash wouldn't say. He wanted us to postpone."

"Maybe he's right."

"Now you're on his side too? What the hell!"

"No… just being cautious, that's all. If something is bothering the Alpha, I mean seriously bothering him, then it might be best to wait for cooler heads."

"Other than the missing cousin, I don't know what else could be going on, but I'll bet the old loner in the desert is responsible for that death."

"Look, I'm not saying no. I'm saying proceed with caution."

"And you? Can you guarantee the witches will be there?"

"I want to say yes. I'm like seventy-five percent sure I can make something happen."

Those were crap odds given the importance of the situation.

"But…"

"But this whole evening could blow up on us." Giselle put her head down a little too hard and banged the desk.

Damien cringed as if waiting to be struck. "Yeah."

Giselle let out an exasperated sigh. "Wonderful. Just wonderful."

Mrs. Freeman called the class to order and instructed them to take out their books.

"Text me before you head out, okay?" Damien said.

"If I even bother." Everything was telling her to abandon this futile plan. If things were truly meant to work out, life wouldn't be throwing so many curve balls at her. Giselle spent the rest of class wondering if she shouldn't just give up. Spend the next two years living with the Hernandez pack and when she was of age, taking off on her own. Gavin had even said being part of a pack was something you felt deep inside. It felt like home. She just couldn't call a warzone her home, no matter how much she liked the combatants.

32

Eight pm rolled around. Dinner was finished; homework too. The family were all deeply entrenched in their nightly routines, having been grounded from the moonlight run thanks to Giselle's earlier escape. She sat in her room, debating what to do, when her cellphone bleated.

Damien: Tonight's a no go. Family won't come. Abort! Abort.

That was a bit melodramatic, she thought. But for some reason, seeing that message tipped her over the edge. If things that were meant to just naturally fell into place, nothing would ever happen. No. It took people willing to go the distance to make thing work that effected real change. And she should take a chance, even if no one showed. Even if it was just her out there, forcing her pack to find the truth, things could be different. All she needed to do was show Martina where her sister was. And the old loner – he could provide the truth about what happened. She didn't need Asher or Damien at all. She could make things happen herself.

She texted Damien back.

Elle: Nope. Not taking no for an answer. Be there.

He responded in seconds.

Damien: No. Seriously. No.

This had to happen tonight, regardless of other people's agendas.

Elle: Going by myself then… to the lone wolf. See ya.

She sent the same message to Asher as well, and then left her phone on the bed. It was up to them if they wanted to come and help clear the air, but she was going to, at the very least, show Martina that her sister was alive… sort of.

Remembering Gavin's warning, she texted one last message to Taylor, who was in the shower.

Elle: Come to the cave, bring the pack. I'm going alone.

That would buy her at least five minutes' head start so no one could stop her, and hopefully ensure someone was close behind, in case Jeffrey was not too happy to see her.

She hopped out the window and scurried through the back gate, shifting as she hit the alleyway, and headed straight for the desert.

Not sure of the reception she would get, or if the lone wolf would give her a chance to explain what she was there for, she ran cautiously toward the creek. In the distance, she heard wolves baying under the moonlight. Her family, possibly, trying to call her back – but she couldn't stop, not when she knew this was right. The statue was Christina. And at the very least, Martina needed to know the truth.

On she pushed herself, through nerves threatening to lock her joints and stop her from going deeper into the desert. She remembered the pain of the lone wolf's teeth in her neck and how that had been his last warning to her to leave. What if he didn't let her explain? No…She couldn't consider those odds at the moment. The need to reveal the truth was all that mattered.

Another wolf cry carried on the wind, but she didn't stop. Giselle pressed onward as the small trickling creek came into view. But she hadn't caught wind of the lone wolf. He had to be around; it was full moon. All wolves would feel the pull and do all they could to change. So, where was he?

The wind shifted, and she caught a strange scent. It might have been the old loner, Jeffery, or it might have just been a dust devil kicking up the musky dirt from the creek. Either way, she needed to press on to the cave. No point in standing still; her fate was sealed.

She picked up her pace again, heading down the creek to where it met the rocky face of the mountain. Ahead she saw the small cave; only this time, there was light coming from within.

That piqued her interest and she quickened her steps. She was almost to the mouth of the cave when she was struck down. Tumbling down into the dirt, she tried to use the momentum and roll back to her paws, but her attacker was on her quicker than she could maneuver. Teeth found flesh beneath her thick fur and sliced like sharpened knives. Pain amplified by the speeding of her heart and fear of death made her cry louder than ever. She squirmed, trying to find her footing and avoid another bite.

It was Jeffrey, that was for sure, but she had no voice to call off his attack. In wolf form, all she could manage was a few yips and barks, mostly in panic. She needed a moment of peace to send the wolf back and transform. Only then would words be of any use. Surely once he knew her purpose he'd relax. In his human form he'd been a grump, but a more reasonable one than the wolf. But finding a way to shift now seemed impossible. Jeffrey attacked with the ferocity of rabid dog, snarling and swiping with his paws, gnashing his teeth when he couldn't find more of her flesh to bite into. Try as she might, she couldn't maneuver quickly enough. At every twist and turn he was there. Every dodge, every duck, each time she narrowly avoided his teeth, he was there again with impossible speed. Jaws snapping and a bite like a bear trap, he was deadly. And he meant business.

He caught her by the neck, and jerking his head side to side, tore out a chunk of fur and some skin as the force of his fury and her own jerky motions sent her off balance, crashing into the creek.

Muddy water was the worst thing she could have landed in. Bleeding from fresh open wounds, every inch of her battered and bruised, the added sting of slime and algae was just the icing on her misery cake. She'd have retched if she weren't sloshing around in the slippery water to find her footing. Jeffrey was already making his move. The moment she got a foothold in the water he pounced on her again, this time hunting for the soft underside of her neck to deliver a killing bite.

Her heart raced. This was not how things were supposed to happen. She didn't even have a moment to howl for her pack – he was too fast and his teeth were too sharp.

He had her pinned on her back, only her snout above water, ready to make the killing blow. Eyes cold as the night, he looked down on her. His mouth opened and Giselle winced, knowing she'd found her end.

But just before he struck, Martina's voice boomed loud as thunder above them. "Let. Her. Go!"

Giselle was too afraid to open her eyes, still expecting to

be struck down and have her throat ripped out. But after a few moments of silence, rather than deliver her end, the wolf above her stepped back.

The pressure lifted and she took in a deep breath as the relief washed over her. Tentatively, still wondering how safe she was, Giselle rolled from her back to her paws. A little unsteady from blood loss and adrenaline running through her body, she eased upwards.

Martina was at her side in a moment, wrapping a blanket around her soaking wet fur. "It's okay. Don't move. Just breathe and relax while I take care of this."

She expected a little anger, after taking off like she did and putting herself into danger, but Martina's words were calm and understanding, with a slight undertone to warn that danger was still present.

Martina turned on the old wolf, stood her ground, and stared him down radiating all the power of an Alpha. "How dare you attack one of my own, on my land? Shift and show yourself to me."

There was no hesitation, no tremble of worry in her voice. She was all Alpha. No. Questions. Asked. And to Giselle's surprise, the old wolf shifted immediately, and lowered his head in submission.

"Jeffrey?" Martina gasped. Her proud stance softened a bit, but she made no move towards him.

"Surprised you recognized me after all these years." The old wolf, now a man, let out a heavy breath and wiped the blood from his mouth.

"How could I forget? Christina…" Martina's voice failed her for a moment. "But that's beside the point. How could you attack a pup?"

"I warned her to stay away. Stupid pup."

She snarled at his condescension.

"Well, she was warned. Twice now."

Martina cast a sidelong glance at Giselle, and Giselle nodded, confirming the truth. A smarter wolf probably would have listened to the warnings. Giselle understood that now more than ever as her wounds stung like fire. But she'd had to come.

"We'll discuss that later." The warning of future punishment was there in Martina's voice, and Giselle would take her lumps later; for now she was so grateful that her life had been spared. Martina turned back on Jeffrey. "What are you doing here?"

The old wolf turned his head away, glancing over at the cave. "I've always been here. This is my home."

"No one lives here. This is open desert."

"I've lived here since everything went down."

Martina's jaw nearly dropped. "Why?" The shock on her face was horrifying.

"Because I said I'd never leave her no matter what." The old wolf sighed. "And I meant it."

Tears formed in the corner of Martina's eyes, but she made no effort to wipe them as they spilled over and ran free down her cheeks. The love she had for her sister, even now, after all the years, made Giselle's heart ache too.

Even crying, Martina still had a stoic look about her face. There was more there under the surface, but the Alpha was holding back as she faced Jeffrey and heard his truth.

In the distance a caravan of headlights came rumbling towards them. Too little too late, Giselle thought. If not for Martina's quick response, Giselle would have been a corpse. She assumed it was Damien's family, the witches, as wolves would have arrived on all fours. And then, a moment later, a chorus of howls confirmed her suspicion. That had to be the Thrace pack. She smiled inwardly, proud to have forced both sides to show up. Even if they were late. Her text message had worked better than she'd hoped.

That left only her own small group missing in action. Where were they, and why so late to the party? Questions better left asked later when the air had been cleared. Giselle refocused on Martina and Jeffrey. Martina still stood her ground while the old wolf looked very much the feeble old man, shivering in the cold without his fur coat. He seemed far less intimidating now.

"Sounds like the cavalry is here," the old wolf said. "Mind if I dress for company?"

"Please do," Martina said, and allowed the old wolf to retreat into his cave. She relaxed her defensive stance and picked up a pile of clothes she must have brought with her in haste to get here.

Giselle found the strength to shift back to her human form, and for the first time ever, it hurt. Her skin pulled tight against her bones, and wounds that should have knitted together during the shift seemed to re-open and trickle fresh blood. Giselle whimpered silently as she attempted and failed to stand.

Martina kneeled down and pulled her into a hug, wrapping the blanket even tighter around Giselle's shivering body. "Why didn't you tell me?"

"I couldn't," was all Giselle could manage to say at the moment. A mix of pain and the inability to explain weeks of confusion, planning, and uncertainty kept the words stuck in the back of her throat.

"These wounds will need herbs to heal, but we'll get you taken care of." She put a hand under Giselle's chin, tipping her head up so their eyes could meet. Where there should have been anger, Martina's eyes were filled with pain and worry. The guilt that swam in Giselle's stomach at that moment made the pain she was feeling all that much worse. Martina's words too, spoken in the calmest of voices, only added to it. "If you'd just come to me with this... Oh, it doesn't matter now. What matters is that you are safe. Pack or not, I am here for you. You have to trust me. Okay? "

"I just wanted to help…" It was work for Giselle to get even those simple words out. And she knew Martina couldn't possibly understand her true meaning yet.

"You can't help, pup." Jeffrey emerged from his den, wearing what must have passed for clothes for him – holey sweat pants that were well past their prime and hardly covered a thing, topped by a shirt so stained it was impossible to tell what the original color must have been. He looked everything like what she expected a hobo to be. "Not your business at all what happened to Christina."

Despite all attempts to remain stoic, at the mention of her sister's name more tears streamed down Martina's cheek. "Please stop saying her name."

"I'll not pretend she's gone, because she ain't!" Jeffrey's voce carried more conviction than it had before.

"What do you mean, she's not?" Martina asked.

"She's here. Just inside. But you won't like what you see. Tell her, Giselle."

Martina looked up, shocked at Jeffrey. "Tell her what?"

"Don't act like you don't know. Your father and that old bastard Thrace…"

"My father did all he could to protect us from—"

Anger gave power to Jeffrey's voice, something reminiscent of the former glory that wolf might have had. He snarled at Martina, "Your father sacrificed your sister to save face."

If Martina's eyes grew any wider they'd have burst from their sockets. "My father…" Her voice trailed off as if she were struck silent with a realization she didn't want to admit.

"Yes." Jeffrey sounded more the Alpha now that Martina. He stared her down, anger and pain filling his eyes. "I watched the whole thing."

The cars that had been slowly rumbling towards them pulled to a stop, and Damien hopped out first. "Giselle," he shouted, head darting around as he searched with weak human eyes in the dark to find her.

"I'm here," Giselle called back to him, attempting to conceal the pain in her voice.

He was at her side in an instant, her knight in flannel armor. "What the hell were you thinking? When I got that text... Thank the Goddess! I'm so happy to see you." His eyes darted all over, visually inspecting her, and stopping every so often as if seeing something a little more interesting.

"Eyes up top, mister." Downplaying her injuries, she attempted to laugh, but that only made her hurt worse.

"Sorry. Just making sure you're all right." He blushed, and thanks to her wolfy night vision, she caught the flush on his cheeks. If she'd been in a better mood, it would have melted her heart.

"That's the question of the night," she huffed, too much in pain to force out a laugh. "Yes. I'm fine. I haven't gone mental or anything, and my wounds will heal soon. Don't worry."

Martina looked confused, casting furtive glances at Damien, but still trying to maintain her focus on Jeffrey. "Did you call the witch here?" The question had been clearly directed at Giselle, but another woman answered before she could.

"The witch has a name," the woman, stepping out of a van answered sharply. "My son tells me we are needed here. It's a matter of life or death?"

Martina turned to address the woman. "Jasmine? It's been far too long."

"So, is everyone old friends here?" Giselle asked. "Because this is going to get pretty confusing if not."

"All people of supernatural heritage are supposed to announce themselves. Common courtesy. So, yes, we are acquainted. But I'm still confused as to why we're all here." Jasmine stepped forward and offered her hand to Martina. "It has been too long."

Behind her, a group of people – witches, Giselle assumed – stood close to their vehicles. Probably waiting for their leader to give an order. The sheer number of them made Giselle a bit nervous. Things could go really well, or terribly, utterly wrong. She hoped for the former.

Jasmine and Martina grasped hands in a very business like manner, neither of them looking as if they were too happy to be doing so, but there was no outward animosity between them. More like annoyance for having the meeting forced on them.

Giselle could see where Damien got his puppy-dog eyes. Jasmine had the kind of look that would probably make any man melt, and a body to match. Tall and slender, she floated rather than walked as she came to meet Giselle. She knelt down, eye level, and offered her hand again. "I've heard nice things about you, lone wolf. Let's make sure they all stay nice."

Was that a warning? She looked to Damien, who simply shrugged and smiled.

"I should kill you all for trespassing on my land." Jeffrey called attention back to himself, trying again to regain his dominance. "None of you are welcome here."

The witches didn't take to kindly to Jeffrey's posturing. They began to come forward, as a pack, toward their leader Jasmine. She held out her hand and stopped them in their tracks. "Answers first, please. Why are we here?"

"No need for hostility, Jeffrey." Martina found her Alpha voice again. "Giselle has a purpose for bringing us here tonight and we're going to let it play out." Martina nodded to Giselle.

She needed to find the strength and get up to say her piece. More than that, she needed to get Jeffrey to bring out Christina. That, more than her words, would reveal the truth.

But before she could find that strength and stand, the wolves that had been howling in the distance began to arrive, coming from both sides. The Thrace family was large – ten wolves had come. Giselle wasn't sure which one was Asher, as they were all dark in color, but she was sure he was in the pack. On the other side were Gavin, the white wolf, and the two girls running at full speed to Martina's side.

"Well, the gang's all here." The power and pride in Jeffrey had faded at the sight of so many more wolves. He huffed and frustrated kicked the dirt. "Let's get whatever this is on the road…"

Giselle mustered the strength to stand. Damien stood with her to provide additional support. "Bring her out, Jeffrey. Show everyone what became of Christina, and see if we can't end this stupidity."

Martina turned on Giselle. "He really does have Christina?"

Giselle nodded, but before she could answer, Mr. Thrace shifted. "There had better be a damn good reason I was called out here." One of his pack members dropped a sack of clothes, and he began to pull on a pair of slacks.

Giselle would have laughed if it didn't hurt so much to move. The thought of an Alpha like him wearing business slacks in the desert was a bit absurd. But she waited patiently for him to dress before she continued.

"Some years ago, your fathers arranged a marriage. One that, for obvious reasons, failed."

"I've heard enough," Mr. Thrace said, and turned an angry eye on one of his wolves. "This is what I had to see? Some kid spouting off about things she couldn't possibly understand."

"You will let her speak, Nathaniel!" Martina's hands were already balling at her sides. She stared down Mr. Thrace like a bull seeing red.

"I don't have to listen to any of this, and I will hold you and your pack responsible for—" Nathaniel Thrace had not even gotten the word out before Gavin stepped up, growling at Martina's side. She too looked ready to shift and fight; Giselle could see hair already sprouting on the back of her neck and shoulders.

"You want a fight, Thrace? Just say the word and we'll settle things like wolves." Martina was positively scary when she went full Alpha.

A wolf shifted into Asher.

"Father, for once in your life, father, listen to someone else talk."

"How dare you speak out against me?" Nathaniel Thrace's hand cocked back for a smack that never landed. Jeffrey, moving at a speed Giselle never thought possible, grabbed it before Mr. Thrace could swing.

"Why don't you let the pups explain? Seems to me they're a bit more in the know than you think." He nodded to Giselle.

"And I should listen to you, why?" Mr. Thrace snarled and tried to pull his arm free, but Jeffrey held tight.

"Because I'll break this arm if I see it fly again without cause."

"Strong words, Lone Wolf. You can't back them up without a pack."

"Care to try me?" Jeffrey growled under his breath. He didn't need to say it, but he had the power of Martina and her pack on his side.

Tension ran thick. Even the witches stepped back in apprehension of a full-on wolf fight. Giselle had intended to bring an end to all the blind rage and fighting between these packs, but the way things were going, they'd all annihilate themselves before the night was over. Everyone looked one hair's breadth from tearing each other into pieces.

"Stop fighting!" Giselle yelled loud enough for her words to echo off the mountain walls. She winced in pain, not realizing how much it took out of her to do that. But she had the attention of everyone at that moment, and the sudden weight of all eyes fell on her. She hesitated, not quite knowing what to say now that they were listening. The murderous glare Mr. Thrace was giving her made her want to shrink back down into the creek where she'd been lying a few moments before. Asher left his father's side and came to join Giselle. He put an arm around her, and that small gesture gave her more strength than she could have hoped for. With a deep breath, she found her voice again. "Look. I'm not going to mince words. All parties here tonight are part of what happened. Part of what started this war, or whatever you want to call it."

The witches mumbled and whispered amongst themselves. Jasmine looked sharply at her son.

Damien spoke up. "Yes, our family too. Listen up. All we want is to make things right." He turned back towards Giselle. "Keep going, you've got their attention."

The show of support from both Damien and Asher worked wonders on her nerves, and even though she was still struggling to keep the pain from her voice, she held her head high and continued. "You've both been at war for years thinking the other side had wronged you, when in fact, both of your parents are the cause. The alliance and marriage were all just for show. None of it was necessary for peace. Just be at peace. How hard is that? The fact is, your parents couldn't see past their own pride, and when the marriage idea failed, they started a war instead. All the lives lost since them are a testament to the stupidity of fighting. I brought you all here, with the help of your children, who are not blinded by pride, to see if we can't change the course of the future of our families. We all live here. We all have to find a way to be at peace."

"Eloquent word for someone like you," Mr. Thrace said, but the spite in his voice was still there.

She wasn't surprised by the backhanded compliment and returned the favor in kind. "Prejudice is your problem, sir. You seem to think everyone is beneath you. Try being less of a bigot."

He looked like he wanted to pounce on her and finish the job Jeffrey had started, but held his ground.

"Make your point, pup, before my patience has run its course."

"I wasn't aware you had any patience." Giselle knew she shouldn't have said it the moment the words left her lips, but couldn't have stopped herself even if she'd thought about it ahead of time.

Nathaniel Thrace lunged forward, but before he could get anywhere near Giselle, Martina shifted and pounced on him. Asher threw himself in front of Giselle, and Damien grabbed hold of her and held her back.

When the dust had settled, Asher had regained his wolf form and was standing guard while Martina held a paw on Mr. Thrace's chest.

Gavin stood at Thrace's head, growling, teeth ready to snap should Martina give a signal. The hairs on the back of his neck were standing near straight, and he looked just as rabid as Jeffrey had earlier when Giselle had been in that same vulnerable position.

"I brought you here for peace… Stop fighting. Stop being assholes. Just… stop!" Giselle's pain sharpened her voice. Damien held her tightly still, and though she was sure he didn't mean to cause her more pain, he was pressing down on her wounds.

He let go as if he knew and took a step back.

Giselle looked at Jeffrey. "Can you please… just bring Christina out?"

Jeffrey shrugged and walked toward the mouth of the cave. "Little help," he grunted, but didn't turn back to see if anyone was coming.

Gavin took the hint and trotted behind Jeffrey, and Asher followed too. The three men, working together, slowly pushed the wolf statue out.

That was it. The missing piece to the puzzle, and the moment it came into view, aggression melted away into awe. Martina stepped off Nathaniel and shifted back to her human form. She retrieved what remained of her clothes that had been shredded by her quick shift moments before and tossed them on. Cautiously, as if afraid, she walked over to the statue, mouth hanging open in disbelief. "She looks… so real."

Words failed Mr. Thrace as well. He stood slowly, dusting off his trousers and shirt, and then walked around the statue twice before finally speaking. "And you are certain this is Christina?"

"There is only one way we'll be sure." Giselle nodded to Damien.

He took the hint and left Giselle's side to return to his family.

"Only someone who cast this kind of spell could reverse it," Giselle began. "We have no way of knowing who did that, but we hope that as our three families are tied to this, that someone may come forward to assist."

She waited as the witches conversed with each other. Gavin shifted and pulled Martina into his arms. She'd held back her emotions for so long, but now the dam burst and the Alpha was sobbing loudly into her husband's chest.

Jeffrey walked over to Giselle. "No matter what happens... you did a good thing, pup."

"So, you won't try to kill me again?" she asked.

He looked her over. Blood had soaked through the blanket she was wearing, and the old wolf's face slacked. "I'm sorry. I truly am. Will you forgive me?"

She should hate him for what he'd done. If he'd been a normal human being, an act like this would have been child abuse. He'd be sent to prison. But the supernatural world worked differently. She could be mad, but she had also been given ample warning. She nodded at the old wolf. "I understand why you did it. Defending your territory is your right. Just remember that we're human too. Try using words before teeth."

"Spoken like a true Alpha. I think you'll make a good one someday."

Giselle wasn't so sure about that, but she was well past arguing anymore. She desperately wanted this whole thing to be done with. Blood loss was making her weak and dizzy. What she needed most was rest. But the witches had not yet come to any decisions.

Asher's father still looked positively murderous. Asher had walked over to talk to him, but the old wolf said nothing in return. She met the Alpha's eyes briefly and felt his anger, but there was no point in pointing out to him that it was all his doing. He could be a good leader without being a tyrannical prick. And for the first time she admitted to herself that if she had to choose a pack, she was glad she had been placed with Martina.

Finally, when Giselle was beginning to lose all hope,

the witches came forward. Jasmine spoke for them. "Rather than reveal the person responsible, we will all join together as one voice to lift the spell."

That was music to her ears. Giselle smiled at Damien, and he in turn winked back at her. No doubt he'd put every ounce of his charm into helping his coven make the right decision. The more time she spent with him, the more she liked that boy. And though she'd tried to ignore it, his affection for her had been genuine right from the start. She looked over at Asher, the hot wolfboy, standing au naturel as many wolves seemed to be comfortable with, and despite his good looks, couldn't find the same affection for him as she'd developed for the witch. Sure he was hot; there was no denying that. But he'd been so aloof. So distant. Even when he'd kissed her, the moment was gone before she could enjoy it.

He must have felt her eyes on him. Asher looked back at her but remained stoic, standing next to his father.

Too bad.

The witches surrounded the wolf statue and began a slow chant, something in another language. She couldn't understand the words, but there was poetry there in the way they spoke. A natural rise and fall, almost like music. As they joined hands, their chants became synchronized as if only one person was speaking with many voices.

Eager to see a real spell in progress, Giselle kept her eyes locked on the statue. She hoped to see flashes of light or sparks or fairy dust... something extraordinary, but nothing even close to what happened.

As if waking from a dream, the statue lost its marble sheen, and the rock faded dully into fur. Slowly, with the sound of popping bone, the wolf began to move. First the head, then a paw, and finally, the poor thing collapsed on the ground.

"Give her a moment," Jasmine said. "She's been frozen for some time. She'll take a bit to warm up."

No one moved at first, whether in fear or from shock, but Jeffrey was not taking the warning to heart. He knelt down next to the wolf lying sleepily on the ground. "My darling, wake up."

Giselle held her breath, waiting with anticipation. The wolf did not move for several minutes. What if the spell had failed? Giselle's heart seized up at the thought of it. She'd never considered that as a possibility and held her breath, praying that wasn't the case.

Jeffrey stroked her fur lovingly, tears of joy spilling unchecked down his cheek, and whispered softly in her ears. "Thank you. Thank you. Oh… thank you."

Then she shifted. The fur faded, and a woman, young, with long dark hair, took shape. She moaned groggily and stretched her arms before sitting up.

"Christina?" Martina whispered cautiously, as if the woman in front of her might disappear if she spoke too loudly.

The young woman turned to face her sister. She was an exact copy of Martina, only younger. "Sister?" Christina said.

Martina joined Jeffrey at her side and pulled her sister in to a hug. "I thought I'd never see you again."

"What happened?" Christina asked, eyes near bulging as she took in the sight of wolves and witches all around her. "Who are all these people?"

"We have a lot to catch up on. But that's for later." Martina pulled back, placing a hand on either side of Christina's face. "I can't believe it. My sister. After all this time." She looked as if she'd never let her go.

Giselle looked over to Mr. Thrace. She expected to see more of his seething anger, but found instead soft eyes staring down at the young Christina. Against her wolf's warning to stay away, she pulled her blanket tight around her and walked over to him. "You loved her, didn't you?" Giselle asked.

Mr. Thrace's jaw tightened as he looked to acknowledge Giselle. "I did, but she was loved by another."

"Did you know what your father had done?"

"No. Not this. I knew he had ordered a curse. I thought that was why Martina had never had children. But never this. I would not have allowed him to do this to Christina." Heartfelt, his words spoke volumes, and gave Giselle a tiny sliver of sympathy for the jilted lover.

Mr. Thrace left Giselle without another word and joined Martina and Christina. He held a hand out to Martina. "For what it is worth, I am sorry for what my father had done."

Martina hesitated before accepting his hand. "Mine too. I believe our children have it right, though. We should call a truce and cast aside the anger."

"I think it in our best interest." Mr. Thrace squeezed her hand once and then released it. "We'll discuss terms after the full moon. I will take my leave now."

"You know where to find me," Martina said, but her attention had already returned to her sister. "We have so much to catch up on."

Christina's confused look faltered as she met the loving eyes of her sister and husband. "I look forward to that. But first, can we run? The moon is calling."

The wolf always has its way. Giselle breathed a sigh of relief. Mission accomplished, and seeing the sisters run off into the hills together was better than she could have hoped for.

Asher surprised Giselle, strolling up with a wry smile that looked so good on him. "You're one resourceful little wolf. And a pretty one, too."

"Are you flirting with me… now?" Still in pain, Giselle fought to hide it from her voice.

"Now that I'm free to do so, yes. I guess I am."

She shook her head. Looking over his shoulder, she saw Damien in the distance. He was talking with his mother, but his eyes kept darting back in her direction.

"I'm flattered, really…" She bit her lip, unsure of what to say.

"But?" Asher's self-assured look faded.

"But Damien flirted with me before he was allowed to…"

"He's a smarter guy than me." Asher's jaw tightened. "But I learn from my mistakes."

"We'll see." Giselle smiled. "Your pack is leaving. You'd better go catch up."

"See you in school tomorrow." There was a hopeful tone in his voice, and she wouldn't deny him hope, but her decision had been made. Damien had not only put in the effort, but had not allowed anything to stop him. That spoke volumes about his intentions.

"See you tomorrow. Bright eyed and bushy tailed." Giselle tried for sarcasm, but failed miserably.

He shifted before trotting off to meet his pack. Mr. Thrace made no further good byes; he shifted and took off without another word.

Giselle felt as if she were ready to collapse on the spot. And as she swooned from exhaustion and blood loss, Damien caught her. "Do I get bonus points for showing up first?"

She giggled. Blood loss had made her more than a little giddy. "I think we'll give you the win tonight. But if you want more points, drive me home. I'm spent."

"Your chariot awaits…" He scooped her up into his arms, shocking her with how easily he carried her. She would have expected something like that from Asher, but not Damien.

"Thank you," she said softly, and snuggled against his chest.

"You deserve all the credit. I didn't think it was possible, but you managed a truce. That's more than anyone has done for this family in years."

"All in a day's work." Giselle allowed him to carry her all the way to a truck. He set her down lightly in the back bed and shouted back to his mother he was taking her home.

"No magical funny business," she managed to say, before finally succumbing to the exhaustion that had taken over.

33

Six months later

Take the picture, damn it, my face is hurting from all this
smiling." Giselle was trying to hold it together, but it
seemed like they'd spent hours posing for the perfect family
picture. How many different ways could you hold your arms
around your sisters' necks? And if one more person blinked,
she was going to wolf out… seriously.

"Language, young lady!" Martina barked, but didn't look
over the camera she was holding.

Giselle growled but held her arms out, around her new
sisters. Everyone had on their plastic smiles as Martina
clicked away, taking photo after photo.

"One more. We need to make every moment today
count!" She was more excited about this than Giselle had
been, and it was supposed to be her special day.

"Just let her have this." Taylor spoke through clenched
teeth so as not to ruin her picture-perfect smile. "She lives
for days like this."

"If I smile any harder, my face is going to freeze like
this," Giselle whimpered, cheeks aching, but held her lips
still.

Diana snorted. "Suck it up, sister. You're stuck with us now. Good or bad."

In the past, Giselle might have been put off by a snarky comment like that, especially when Diana said it with such enthusiasm, but today it only helped her find the strength to keep up her smile for one more picture.

"Hold on. Someone blinked." Martina groaned. "And there's too much sun. How about we move over by the back gate?"

The three girls groaned in unison. "Save me from picture hell," Giselle mouthed to Damien, who'd spent the last five minutes snickering with the rest of the men standing by the grill. If she'd hoped for him to save her, she was out of luck. Some things were beyond the witch's power.

A knock at the gate startled Giselle. She hadn't been expecting more company, and by the smell that accompanied the sudden sound, more wolves were about.

Taylor skipped over and opened the gate, greeting Asher and his father with a friendly smile. "Glad you could make it."

Nathaniel, in his standard business professional dress, looked a bit too formal for a back yard barbeque, but he came bearing gifts, so Giselle reined in the snarky thoughts in her head.

In the last few months, the two packs had called a truce and had been working hard to get over the years of animosity. And Mr. Thrace, despite his usual abrasive nature, had civilly attended joint moonlight runs. There was still a bit of tension among them, but time and a mutual desire for peace was helping to heal the wounds.

"Where should I set this?" Nathaniel asked, already walking towards the table stacked with gifts.

"Thank you. Over there is fine," Martina said as an afterthought. She was a little preoccupied with camera settings and taking test shots at the gate. "There's beer and soda in the cooler. Help yourself."

Asher joined the girls and pulled Giselle into a bear hug she wasn't expecting. "So it's official now, eh? You're a pack animal?"

She had to wait for him to set her down and let go before she could speak. "You got any problems with that?" She gave him a playful stink-eye, calling back the memories of his first warning to her.

"None." He laughed. "You're part of a good pack now."

Not that she needed the confirmation, but hearing it from him was nice. He smiled at her with those gorgeous eyes and she could see the spark was still there between them, but he'd missed that opportunity. Giselle glanced past him to Damien, who was casually chatting with Gavin at the grill, and smiled. "You're right. I am part of a good pack."

Asher took the hint and bowed out gracefully, turning his attention to Taylor, who was all too eager to chat with him.

They'd make a cute couple, Giselle thought to herself. Taylor, with her impeccable taste in clothing and social standing in school, would complement the Thrace pack nicely.

She was about to follow her nose over to the tempting smell of cooking meat on the grill when Martina called out again for everyone to line up for pictures.

Heaving a sigh, she stood in line again and flashed her best 'take-the-damn-picture smile.

"Okay. I think I got it." Martina waved her hand in the air triumphantly.

Giselle let out a sigh of relief.

"Now. One more with the whole family… Damien, will you take the picture for us?" Martina didn't wait for an answer. She tossed the camera over to the witch and headed for Giselle and the rest of the group. "Okay, Christina and Jeffrey, you two back left. Gavin, honey, over here with me. Giselle, you stay centered. Everyone…. Cheese!"

One more picture and Giselle was seriously going to lose it. Especially with the delicious smell of steak cooking on the grill. They were so close she could practically taste the meat. It was all she could do to hold her inner wolf at bay. The sizzle, the wafting aroma… and those spices. Gavin had some secret steak-rub that just made her mouth water. Her new dad was a genius with the grill. If she wasn't careful, they'd get pictures of her drooling.

Focus. Smile. One. More. Picture.

Aside from the barrage of pictures, the day had been perfect. She'd spent the morning in court, where the judge had awarded her a brand new family, they'd celebrated with sweets and all the sugary toppings they could pile on at her favorite yogurt shop; and now, the entire family had gathered, including her boyfriend, Damien, for a welcome home celebration.

Damien gave the thumbs up and the group broke up.

"Please say we're done with pictures," Giselle groaned at Martina. "I'm starving."

"Don't you be a spoil sport. This is an important day." Martina gave her a smile to counteract the bite in her voice. "For everyone here. You gained a family, but we also gained something important."

"What?"

"You." She pulled Giselle into a tight hug. "I could never have babies, so for me, adoption is just as important as any birthing day would be. And you" – she pulled back and, placing a hand on either side of Giselle's face, looked down into her new daughter's eyes – "are my newest baby. I will love you until my dying breath."

Eye contact like this was overwhelmingly uncomfortable, but not in the dominant Alpha sense. The sentiment was not lost on Giselle. She'd always wanted a mom. And now she had one. She was part of a family and a pack that wanted her. And more than that, loved her for what she was. It was her dream come true!

Gone were the days of hiding her condition. No more would she ever have to worry about being sent away for being different. She was home. For good.

And that feeling was beyond words.

She broke eye contact, burying her face into Martina's shoulder, partially to avoid showing the world there was tears in her eyes, but another, much bigger part enjoying the feeling of having a mom to hug.

In the end, she realized, things that were meant to be didn't come from sitting around and wishing. It took a little bit of magic and a whole lot of fighting for what you want.

And now that she had it, she was never letting go.

Other Books by Katie Salidas

The Immortalis Series
Becoming a Vampire is easy. Living with the
condition is the hard part.
Carpe Noctem
Hunters & Prey
Pandora's Box
Soulstone
Dark Salvation

Olde Town Pack
Werewolf romances to make your pulse race
and heart pound.
Moonlight
Mated
Being Alpha

Chronicles of the Uprising
Dystopian thrillers with a Paranormal twist.
Dissension
Complication
Revolution
Transition
Retribution
Annihilation

Little Werewolf Series
A Coming of Age Wolf Shifter Adventure.
Pretty Little Werewolf
Curious Little Werewolf
Fearless Little Werewolf

About the Author

Katie Salidas is a best-selling author known for her unique genre-blending style.

Host of the Indie Youtube Talkshow, Spilling Ink, nerd, Doctor Who fangirl, Las Vegas Native, and SuperMom to three awesome kids, Katie gives new meaning to the term sleep-deprived.

Since 2010 she's penned four bestselling book series: the Immortalis, Olde Town Pack, Little Werewolf, and the RONE award-winning Chronicles of the Uprising. And as her not-so-secret alter ego, Rozlyn Sparks, she is a USA Today bestselling author of romance with a naughty side.

Facebook
www.facebook.com/pages/Katie-Salidas-Author/214780936916
Web
www.katiesalidas.com/
Twitter
twitter.com/QuixoticKatie
Email
KatieSalidas@gmail.com
SpillingInk
www.youtube.com/c/spillinginkshow

Join the Paranormal Posse
Readers and get exclusive updates and connect directly with Katie Salidas!
www.facebook.com/groups/ParanormalPosse/

Please Review

Your opinion matters! When people first look at a book, beyond the description and the cover, they pay close attention to what others like you have to say.

If the book is getting overwhelmingly good or bad reviews, it can weigh heavily on that readers decision whether or not to click that purchase button.

It does not have to be a book report.
It does not have to be 5 stars. I would never ask for any special favoritism.

A book review is simply sharing what you thought of the book. It answers two very simple questions:

Did you like it?
Would you recommend it to someone else?

That's it. Your opinion matters. Most importantly to me, because I want to ensure you are enjoying the books I write. But beyond my hope for your satisfaction, the review you write caries great weight in the publishing realm as well. It can quite literally make or break a book.

So, here I am, groveling at your feet.
If you have read one (or more) of my books, would you do me the greatest of honors and leave a review?